TITANIC

Ghosts of Southampton Book 1

ID JOHNSON

CONTENTS

For my mom, the one I knew and treasured as a little girl so many years ago.

CHAPTER 1

She had not expected to find herself standing here aboard the largest cruise liner in the world, a Third Class passenger, staring back at the ever shrinking dock of her native Southampton, wondering where she was headed, how she would get there, and whom she would become upon the other side.

Yet, here she was at midday on a cold, windy April 10, staring out at a myriad of faces she, thankfully, did not recognize, wearing someone else's dress, her hair down and billowing in the breeze, leaving everything behind, starting anew.

Well, perhaps not everything. The fresh wounds mingled with old scars, both figuratively and literally, and she couldn't help but think about the baggage she carried with her, despite the one small carpetbag she had stowed below deck earlier before coming aboard to fake a smile and wave at strangers. It would take some time to let the lingering memories fade, let the wounds heal, let the scars dissipate. At least now, on this new journey, she was compelled to breathe a small sigh of relief, knowing there was little chance that anyone with knowledge of her former existence, with the exception of the woman standing next to her and her young family, would likely be within a thousand miles of her location in just a few days' time. The acceptance of this information was enough to coax the forced smile to meet her eyes. Perhaps she would have some semblance of peace at last and the opportunity to start again.

That was her initial thought, anyway, until she felt the piercing sting of a penetrating gaze from over her right shoulder and glanced up to realize at least one of her problems had followed her after all.

Gasping in recognition, she turned quickly, directing her stare back at the crisp blue water below her. Though she had not intended to cause a stir, she caught the attention of her companion at her side. With an annoyed smirk, Kelly gave her only partial attention, continuing to wave with one hand as she held her baby against her shoulder. "Meg? What could possibly be the matter now?" she asked through clenched teeth, in her thick Irish accent, bouncing the impatient babe as she did so. "We're launchin'. You can't possibly still be worried that we've been followed."

She was very much aware of the fact that Kelly was no longer obligated to tolerate her paranoia and that the shift in their relationship would allow her a looser tongue were she so inclined to begin to vocalize her disposition, not that their previous arrangement had ever been much of a hindrance to Kelly's self-expression. Nevertheless, Meg's current state of being unsettled was not at all unwarranted, and the weight of those green eyes still bore through the back of her skull; she could feel it. "He's here!" she replied, gesturing only slightly for her friend to look up at the deck above them.

The annoyance was still very detectable in Kelly's tone. She did not even bother to turn her head. "What do you mean he's here?" she asked, the lilt of her brogue accent coming through even more with the perturbed nature of the statement.

Meg sighed. "Up there. On the First Class Deck. He's on the boat!"

Kelly's smile was completely gone now. Her youngest daughter fussed a bit, and she shifted her to the other shoulder. "How can he possibly be here?" she asked. "He had an appointment with your uncle just this afternoon. He wouldn't cancel. He wasn't scheduled to be aboard. Are you sure?"

"Look!" Meg insisted. As Kelly began to turn around, Meg's small, well-groomed hand sprang out to catch her shoulder. "Be more discreet!" she implored. "I don't want to draw any more attention to myself! He's already looking at us!"

It was Kelly's turn to sigh now. "Jesus, Mary, and Joseph," she mumbled. "Here, take the baby," she insisted, shoving the child over to her friend, who opened her arms just in time. Kelly pretended to be looking for someone along the lower deck promenade where they stood. By now, her curious behavior had drawn the attention of her husband and older daughter who stood next to them, but neither were yet inclined to ask exactly what was going on. Instead, Daniel turned back to his four-year-old daughter, Ruth, whose fiery red hair, the same shade as her mother's, wafted in the wind, as she made endless inquiries about the other boats moored at the White Star Dock, one of which, *The New Yorker*, had gone a bit rogue only a few moments ago.

Kelly, eventually, turned her attention to the deck above them as instructed, and after surveying the situation much longer than Meg was comfortable with, she finally turned back around. "You're hallucinatin', darlin'. I see plenty of handsome rich men, but I don't think your betrothed is among them."

"What?" Meg replied, eyes crinkled in disbelief. "Yes, he is. I saw him with my own eyes." Without giving it much thought, she turned and looked directly back at the spot where he had been standing. Kelly was right. He wasn't there, or if he was, he was obscured by the hundreds of other passengers attempting to gain a view of *The New Yorker* being towed back to dock. "He was right there, I swear!" Meg insisted, her shawl flipping about as she swirled back to face her friend.

"Keep your voice down," Kelly warned, glancing around again. "Or else you really will have unwanted attention."

Meg wanted to argue, though she knew Kelly was right. With a huff, she turned back to face the rippling blue surface beneath them. Despite Kelly's insistence that she was only seeing a manifestation of one of her most prevalent fears, she was quite certain she had, in fact, seen her fiancé staring down at her from above. She would recognize those stunning green eyes anywhere. While the fact that he had been looking directly at her was cause to think he knew who she was and had recognized her, despite the oddness of their prior arrangement and her guise, she could only hope that he had not detected her deception.

Thankfully, they were aboard the largest passenger ship ever built where there was an understood arrangement that First Class passengers and Steerage were not to interact. The likelihood that she would encounter him again was highly implausible.

⚜

"THE OCEAN'S OUT THERE," Jonathan Lane probed with a small nudge.

With a slight blush, Charlie Ashton pulled his attention away from the young lady who had caught his eye and shrugged. "Sorry," he mumbled. "I was lost in thought."

Jonathan shook his head knowingly. "I understand this isn't where you expected to be, but we may as well make the most of it. It isn't everyday one finds himself on the maiden voyage of the greatest vessel ever to sail the seven seas."

Charlie laughed, picking up on the sarcasm in Jonathan's tone. "God Himself could not sink this ship," he replied, quoting the often repeated phrase.

"Aye, but *The New Yorker* might," Jonathan stated, gesturing at the wayward steamship floating aimlessly away from the docks. "Come on, let's go over here where we can get a better look," he insisted, placing his hand on Charlie's shoulder and guiding him across the deck.

With one more glance at the Third Class passengers below, Charlie complied, despite the paradox in the situation; Jonathan was his liegeman after all. However, given his current disposition, he was inclined to acquiesce. Beautiful girls were nothing but trouble, regardless of station. Of that, he was quite certain. Best to leave the woman with the haunting blue eyes and long blond tresses behind, as he had been so recently abandoned, and follow his manservant in the pursuit of adventure.

⚜

HOURS LATER, lying on an uncomfortable bunk bed in the bowels of the ship, one arm tucked beneath her head, staring up at the unsightly underbelly of the bunk above her, memories invaded Meg's thoughts. Despite the fact that she should be focused on the future, where they were headed, what she would do next, who she would become, the ghosts of the past clung to her thoughts, and she could not shake them.

Kelly and Daniel had taken Ruth back to the Third Class promenade deck once their youngest daughter, Lizzy, who was just eight months old, had fallen asleep, and Meg had insisted on staying with her while the rest of the family set out to hopefully catch a glimpse of Cherbourg. Meg had visited France many times, Kelly at her side as her lady-in-waiting, but the young girl and her father had never left England, and though Daniel's exuberance was somewhat muted, Ruth was bubbling over with excitement. She had been completely wound up all morning, ever since her parents finally revealed their destination to her, and several attempts at rocking Lizzy to sleep had been spoilt by her bigger sister bouncing around the diminutive cabin.

Meg glanced across the small space to the sleeping baby, whose hair was a slightly lighter shade of red than the fiery hue of the other ladies in her family, her father's light coloring seeping in a bit to produce strawberry-blonde locks. Lizzy sighed, her mouth instinctively sucking a few times before she swatted at her nose and stuck her thumb between her thin, pale pink lips. How she wanted to stretch a hand across and brush the hair off of the sweet child's forehead! But she dared not risk awakening the precious darling. Instead, Meg returned her focus back to the underside of the bunk above her, absently twirling a lock of golden-blonde hair as she did so.

The idea of her own baby had crossed her mind several times, this past year especially. Though at first the idea of becoming a mother had been considered as a malicious testimony to what would be her most scandalous transgressions, once she was certain she would soon have an independent life of her own, she began to let the possibility invade her thoughts frequently and realized just how much she longed for her own child. At twenty, she could have easily been considered past her prime by many members of her class if she had not been engaged to marry for these past three years to one of society's most elite bachelors. For one reason or another, the wedding was pushed off—as was every planned encounter—until Meg's mother had put her foot down at last and insisted that the nuptials occur before Meg's twenty-first birthday in September or else. Meg was never quite sure what her mother's "or else" would be in this instance. After all, most of the stalling of the years had actually been instigated by Meg herself, and Mildred Westmoreland certainly had no power or control over the Ashtons, but whatever she had told John and Pamela Ashton of New York high society had been sufficient, and Charlie had embarked on a trip across the Atlantic to meet her in person at last.

But that never happened, and now here she was in the Steerage quarters of a passenger liner headed for Charlie's hometown, buried beneath the same socialites and high class ladies her mother so insisted she emulate.

And she had the stature to do so, despite the fact that the funding for such a parody was written on rubber banknotes, any semblance of cash in the coffers diminishing quickly over the years after her father's death. In her mother's eyes, however, none of that would matter once she wed Charlie. Then, there would be money again, and the family name would be restored. Charlie would take over her father's company as well, as part of the agreement, and her uncle (even the thought of him made Meg shudder) would retire, leaving whatever was left of her father's empire in much better hands.

None of that would happen now. The sigh that escaped Meg's lips was almost as restless as the one Baby Lizzy had released moments ago. The choices she had made, the recent ones as well as the rebellious ones of her former youth, had all compiled, bringing her here. Despite the uncertainty of what lie ahead, she was certain of one thing: if this boat could take her away from those who had imprinted her soul with the black stains that lingered there now, then the hesitations of her journey were well-worth the anxiety she currently felt.

And yet, she could not help but ponder the inexplicable idea that Charlie Ashton was also aboard the *Titanic*, which could easily end her entire charade and bring the newly constructed scaffolding of hope crashing down around her.

CHAPTER 2

The First Class stateroom Charlie Ashton occupied had come at a considerable price, but when he booked his passage aboard the RMS *Titanic* on the morning of its maiden voyage, he had been pleasantly surprised that the famous ocean liner even had availability in its most luxurious accommodations. Jonathan had returned from booking the fair stating that J.P. Morgan, the owner of the vessel, had recently cancelled his own reservation (a possible omen that had caused Charlie to raise his eyebrows) which had left one of the finest staterooms available. Despite the fact that the very owner had determined not to make the maiden voyage, Charlie's desperation to leave England had led him to board the ship, the idea that perhaps the *Titanic* was not as unsinkable as previously mentioned only a drifting thought in an over-crowded mind.

Staring at the frothing waters below as the disturbance of the vast hull made her way through otherwise placid seas, he couldn't help but reflect on the situation that had led him here. He had always gained attention from admiring women, frequently unwanted attention, though occasionally a girl would catch his eye. However, he had known ever since he was a youth that he would eventually wed Mary Margaret Westmoreland. His father had explained the situation to him shortly after Mary Margaret's own father had died several years ago, how John Ashton had made a promise to his long-time friend and business partner, Henry Westmoreland, that he would watch after his only child. Despite some initial trepidation and a bit of a rebellious stage, Charlie came to understand the value of giving one's word, of honoring friendship, of upholding obligations. It was a motto his father had instilled in him long ago, one that he had no intention of ever turning his back on. That was why it was so incredibly difficult for him to understand how others could take such commitments so lightly.

Resting his forearms on the railing that separated him from the bitterly cold abyss below, he ran a hand through his short brown hair and gave an audible sigh. He knew Jonathan would be coming in soon, prepping him for the possibility of friendly business opportunities with other high class members of the First Class elite. The idea of shooting the breeze with the likes of J. J. Astor and Ben Guggenheim seemed incredibly taxing under the present circumstances to say the least. They were both fine gentlemen, as were most of his acquaintances aboard the vessel, but they were also all very much aware that he was not scheduled to be amongst them, which would lead to questions and the inevitable inquiry as to Miss Westmoreland's location.

He heard the door behind him open but did not turn in reply to Jonathan's offered greeting of, "Good morning," as he was not convinced it was such. After a pause, the slightly older man, dressed in a fine suit for such an ordinary day, inquired, "Will you be having breakfast in your room, or shall we venture out among our fellow passengers this morning?"

Charlie straightened to his full height. At six-foot-two, he was quite tall, and he had to lower his gaze several inches to meet Jonathan's eyes. "Coffee—here—will suffice," he replied.

Jonathan crossed his arms as Charlie sunk back down, hands splayed apart on the rail. "Don't you think it will do you some good to get out? Talk to some people? Explore the ship?" he probed.

Despite having served as his valet these past few years, Jonathan had become more of a friend than a servant, and Charlie relied on him for more than just fetching needed items and laying out clothing. Jonathan was as levelheaded and intelligent as most of Charlie's associates. In fact, Jonathan had even attended college for a few semesters before funding failed him, and he was forced to find employment. It was his sharp eye for detail and his charismatic personality that had caused Charlie to choose him from several applicants, and they had formed a bond almost instantly. Having grown up with only a sister, Charlie had always wished for a brother, and he had found that camaraderie at last with Jonathan, at the age of twenty-one. Now, two years later, Jonathan knew him better than anyone else, and he was generally inclined to listen to his advice.

But not today. The thought of dancing through the charade of facades was nauseating. "No thank you," Charlie replied in a quiet, yet decisive voice.

Jonathan knew the tone well and only nodded in acceptance. After a moment, he simply rested his hand on his friend's shoulder briefly before walking almost silently back into the stateroom to fetch the requested coffee.

࿓

"You look pretty pale. Are you sure the rockin' isn't gettin' to you?" Kelly asked, eyeing Meg over breakfast in the Third Class Dining Hall. Daniel had volunteered to get up early with the girls for breakfast and more exploration, leaving Kelly and Meg to have the morning to themselves.

Meg looked down at the dry toast and banana she had absently placed on her plate a few moments ago from the *ala carte* choices. Even though the *Titanic* was the largest passenger vessel ever built, there was still some swaying involved, and Meg was slightly inclined toward seasickness. She could emphatically say, however, that the churning in her stomach had nothing to do with motion sickness. "It's not that," she replied quietly. "It's happening again."

Kelly gave a sympathetic sigh and placed her hand on top of her friend's. "I'm sorry, darlin'," she said. "The same one?" she probed, glad to have the opportunity to discuss the situation without the distraction of small, sticky fingers.

Meg nodded, hesitating to speak aloud for fear the authenticity of verbalizing her thoughts would overwhelm her. A clattering of dishes across the crowded room jarred her a bit, and she caught Kelly's concerned expression. "I guess I thought leaving would make the nightmares stop. And that first night, in the hotel, it did. But now.... I don't want to think about it," she replied, her voice trailing off.

Kelly squeezed her hand, nodding her head, her red, disheveled locks dancing as she did so. "He can't hurt you now, Meg. He's in the past. Now, all you have is a bright future to look forward to."

Meg nodded, withdrawing her hand and breaking off a small corner of the toast before sliding it across the plate and brushing the crumbs from her fingers. "I'm just... afraid things won't turn out the way we planned...."

"They will," Kelly insisted, cutting her off. "You'll see. Once we get to America, everything will be wonderful, just liked we talked about."

"But what if... what if someone recognizes me? What if they wire my mother and tell her where I am?"

Kelly shook her head. "That won't happen. There are only a handful of First Class passengers who've even met you, and the chances that you will run into any of them are highly unlikely."

Meg knew what she said was true, yet she wasn't convinced she had nothing to worry about. However, she hadn't even begun to voice her true concerns. With even more reluctance in her voice, she continued. "What if we get to America, and I can't find a job. I'm not qualified to do anything. Or worse, I realize I really am a spoiled rich girl who can't do without the finer things in life."

Kelly guffawed. "You know that's not the case," she insisted. "You've never been one of them, Meg. You've always scoffed at their holier-than-thou ways. I know you can find work. Your embroidery is impeccable. You can play the piano beautifully."

"Is there high demand for young ladies with those skills in New York City?" Meg snickered, sipping the lukewarm beverage in her mug that was reputedly coffee.

Kelly glared at her a moment before continuing. "I'm just sayin' you have skills. We'll find a way for you to make a living. In the meantime, you know you can stay with Daniel and me for as long as you need to. I'm sure he'll find work. He has years of experience as a carpenter, and

I have every intention of findin' placement in one of those snooty New York housewife's service."

"Perhaps your new employer will not be as much the slave driver as your last," Meg jested, finding some humor at last.

Kelly chuckled. "It would be difficult to find someone as harsh and ridiculing as you," she teased. "It'll be fine," she assured her friend, resting her calloused hand on the sleeve of her own dress, now worn by her former mistress. "You're just worried because... it's not quite how you planned."

As Kelly's voice trailed off, Meg pursed her lips, bracing herself against unwanted tears. She attempted to push thoughts of the one Kelly had alluded to aside, but it did her no good, and she soon felt a familiar sting at the corners of her eyes.

"I'm sorry," Kelly said in the same soothing tone she used to comfort her own children. "I didn't mean to..."

"No, it's okay," Meg insisted, dabbing at her eyes with her napkin. "You're right. It just seems harder because I always assumed he'd be with me."

"I know," Kelly replied, smoothing Meg's hair. "I'm sorry, darlin'."

Meg nodded in acknowledgement of her friend's concern before saying, "It's just as well, I guess. If he was going to leave, at least he did it before I booked his passage to America."

Kelly offered a sympathetic smile. "Well, good riddance is what I say," she finally declared. "You don't need the likes of that two-faced, lowly gobshite, I reckon."

Despite herself, Meg began to laugh. "The further we sail from home, the more prominent your accent becomes, Kel."

Kelly shrugged. "I think it's more likely due to the fact that I feel I can finally be my own person without the weight of your mum and uncle breathin' down my neck at every turn," she explained. After a brief moment, she added, "Maybe you should think on that a bit, love."

Meg considered her statement. "Perhaps you're right," she agreed. *If only I knew how....*

"Now, come on. If you're done pickin' at that toast, let's go up on deck and get some fresh air, see if we can find them wee lasses of mine and my lovin' husband."

CHAPTER 3

I t had taken some probing, but eventually, Charlie had agreed to join Jonathan for some fresh air outside on one of the boat's many promenades. However, a compromise had been negotiated; rather than sauntering about amidst the over-dressed, overly formal members of First Class, Charlie had insisted on traveling down to one of the lower decks where the pressures of sophistication would be replaced with an air of excitement at the journey. Happy to be leaving the cabin, Jonathan agreed, and they made their way to C Deck where mostly Third Class passengers could leave the cramped quarters of Steerage for some fresh air and a view of the ocean.

As they ambled about, discussing the various features of the vessel, Charlie was reminded of how fortunate he was to have such a scholarly valet. Jonathan had done quite a bit of research about the boat before they boarded. Likewise, he soaked up information from overheard conversations and discussions with other gentlemen of his position. The result was a virtual encyclopedia of facts on almost every subject, the present topic of the esteemed RMS *Titanic* notwithstanding.

"The top speed is about twenty-six knots, or so they say," he was explaining as they walked along near the railing, dodging overly-jubilant children who occasionally darted by, "though I would be surprised if we ever got it quite up to that speed."

"That is rather fast," Charlie agreed, his hands deep in his trouser pockets. "And how much faster is that than the *Majestic*?"

"Oh, much faster. The *Majestic* only travels about twenty knots, though the *Lusitania* is just as fast as *Titanic*. Of course, Ismay was building a ship for luxury, not just speed. I think he got it," Jonathan continued.

Charlie nodded, his thoughts elsewhere, though he was listening. Not only was he preoccupied with haunting thoughts of Mary Margaret Westmoreland, the vision of the blonde woman he had seen on the decks below at their initial launch yesterday also began to play across his mind. He pushed all of those thoughts aside, not wanting to waste what small level of concentration he currently had available on unnecessary musings as he refocused on what Jonathan was saying. "Yes, that's true. Luxury was certainly Mr. Bruce Ismay's focus. And he and Thomas Andrews did a top-notch job of reaching a new standard, that's for certain," he agreed, considering his personal accommodations and the aesthetics of the promenade they were visiting. "By the looks of it, even Third Class passengers are quite comfortable."

"Yes, indeed," Jonathan agreed, smoothing back his dark hair behind his ear. "They even have individual cabins." Glancing down over the railing at the decks below momentarily, Jonathan looked up, and then back down again. "However," he muttered, still surveying the area, "I don't believe there are enough lifeboats for all of these people, and the passages below D Deck are rather confusing. Since most of the Steerage accommodations are below D Deck that could be problematic in an emergency."

Charlie raised his eyebrows, considering Jonathan's words carefully. Despite the assurances of the White Star Line, he was, by nature, a cautious person. Nevertheless, he had other things on his mind. Laughing he patted Jonathan on the arm and said, "Don't worry. This boat is unsinkable, right?"

Jonathan returned the chuckle. "Right," he agreed. "Why bother with lifeboats at all?"

As they continued, however, Charlie eyed the frigid water below, and it wasn't just thoughts of freezing temperatures that sent a slight chill up his spine. Something about Jonathan's words seemed too familiar to him, almost like *de ja vu*, and he began to realize every time someone mentioned the implausible idea that the *Titanic* might sink, he couldn't help but wonder if they were tempting their fate.

৩৯৩

SHE WAS GONE! She had been here one moment, giggling at her mother's scarf as it floated above her in the breeze, the next she had vanished. Frantic, Meg looked up and down the promenade, attempting to catch a glimpse of that flame of hair somewhere one direction or the other; she did not see Ruth anywhere.

Daniel and Kelly had decided to return to the cabin to lay Lizzy down for a nap and take a little break themselves, and Meg had insisted she could keep an eye on Ruth, who wasn't done playing just yet, while they did so. Even though Daniel and Kelly had been married for almost five years now, they seldom spent any time alone. He worked long hours as a carpenter, and she was on call twenty-four hours a day, six days a week, taking care of Meg's needs and anything else her mother assigned her. Once the girls were born, Mrs. Westmoreland had agreed to let Daniel move into Kelly's quarters, but before that time, she only lived with her husband on her day off, which made it very difficult to start a family. Now that Meg was in a situation where she could make some of that up to her friend, she was inclined to do so. However, now that their daughter was missing, and Meg was certain she had somehow managed to tumble into the Atlantic Ocean, she had no idea how she could ever face her friends again.

In desperation, she picked a direction, and shot off, hoping she chose correctly and that she would find the missing four-year-old safe and sound. In a rush, with a panicked expression on her face, she parted strolling families and couples, who leapt out of her way as if she had the plague. "Ruth!" she shouted, peering between knees and behind benches. "RUTH! Where are you?" she shouted.

It wasn't until she rounded a corner that she saw the child, and it was hardly at knee level either. Meg gasped in horror when she realized precisely whom the small child had befriended. There, across the promenade, leaning against the railing, having quite the animated discussion with her little charge, was none other than Charles J. Ashton, his strong arms holding the tot up where she could see out across the sea.

Taking a deep breath, Meg proceeded, knowing she had no choice but to retrieve Ruth, though she was ashamed to admit thoughts of slowly backing away crossed her mind. The crew would determine who her parents were eventually, wouldn't they? Charlie would keep her safe until Kelly and Daniel could come and get her, no doubt. Pushing those thoughts aside, and praying that he did not recognize her or ask any questions, she marched onward, trying to focus on the child and avoid those green eyes at all cost.

"Ruth!" she admonished, "there you are! Aunt Meg has been looking everywhere for you, sweetheart."

Ruth hung her head only slightly before meeting Meg's eyes and saying, in her angelic baby voice, "The scarf blew away!"

"Oh, my," Meg said, shaking her head. "Next time, wait for Aunty Meg, darling." She opened her arms and Ruth came to her, still clutching the scarf in her balled up fist.

"I'm sorry, Aunty Meg," she replied with a slobbery kiss on the cheek.

"It's okay, baby," Meg assured her. "You're safe. We should get you back to your mummy. Let's thank the nice man first, all right?"

As Ruth turned to face Charlie, her arms opened again, and she shot back to him, much to his surprise. "Thank you, Uncle Charlie!" she gushed, wrapping her arms around his neck."

Laughing at her spontaneity, Charlie replied, "You're welcome, Ruth. I'm glad your aunt found you. Now, here you go, back to Aunt Meg, and then off to see Mummy."

Without looking directly at him, Meg took Ruth back and said, "Thank you. She just disappeared."

"Not a problem," Charlie offered, patting Ruth gently on the back. "We were just looking for some dolphins, and then we were going to go see if one of the stewards could help us find her parents."

"She's been looking for dolphins most of the morning," Meg

explained, looking at Ruth instead of the man she was speaking to. It occurred to her that, if Charlie had recognized her, he likely would have said something by now. Since he hadn't, chances were he had no idea that he was talking to the woman he had been engaged to for three years. Though she was relieved that her rouse had not been discovered, she dare not tarry and continue to push her luck. "Well, thank you again, sir," she said, not sure whether she should offer her hand, curtsy, or simply nod. She was not yet used to being a Third Class citizen.

If he picked up on her awkwardness, it didn't show. "Oh, please, call me Charlie," he said, though he didn't offer his hand. "And this is my friend Jonathan," he continued.

Meg hadn't even noticed the other man until that second when he stepped to Charlie's side and said, "How do you do, Miss...?"

She froze. She met this stranger's dark brown eyes and noticed the inquisitive stare immediately. The expression on his face reminded her that he had asked a question—one for which she had no answer. She stammered, pondering how to reply.

"She's Aunty Meg," Ruth reminded them, bringing a laugh from everyone, even Meg who was still panicking.

"That's right. I'm Aunty Meg," she confirmed. "And I'm afraid we must be going. Thanks again for your assistance," she repeated, and then, just as she was about to walk away, so close to an escape, she glanced up, as if her eyes were no longer under her control, and she looked straight into those penetrating green eyes. She gasped, turned, and pulled a struggling Ruth away. What she saw there was not recognition and disdain as she had feared, but kindness and intrigue. She began to realize she didn't really know Charlie Ashton at all—and perhaps she wanted to.

Charlie watched as Meg and a waving Ruth disappeared into the crowd, a small smile creeping up at the corners of his mouth. He knew that Jonathan was staring at him in anticipation of an explanation, but he let him wait a bit longer before he finally said, "That was her."

Jonathan's arms were open, his hands palm up in a questioning gesture. "Her who?" he asked, clearly lost.

Charlie rested his elbows on the boat railing behind him. "Her," he replied. "The girl. From yesterday." Jonathan was still clueless, and Charlie was a bit amused at watching his friend attempt to connect the pieces. "Don't you remember yesterday when the boat launched, and you were trying to get my attention? I was staring at her."

Recognition finally washed over Jonathan's face. "Oh, I see," he replied, stepping forward to rest his forearms on the railing. "I guess I didn't realize you were staring at someone in particular. Now I know why..." he muttered.

"Yes, she's pretty amazing," Charlie agreed.

Jonathan looked at him, eyebrows raised in bewilderment. "Since when does Charles Ashton actually admit when he finds a woman attractive?" he inquired.

Charlie shrugged. "That was... before. Now... it doesn't matter so much."

"You never know," Jonathan reminded him, "Miss Westmoreland might show up. She might deposit herself right back into your life. No one called anything off."

"I know," Charlie assured him, turning to face him. "She's not... whatever is going on with Mary Margaret, she made her intentions clear—three times. Even my father can understand that. I appreciate how he values keeping promises, but there's something to be said for family pride as well, you understand?"

"Of course I do," Jonathan agreed. "And I have no doubt Mr. Ashton will be appalled at her behavior once you give him the full story. But in the meantime, I'm just saying, don't start thinking of yourself as being an officially eligible bachelor."

Charlie nodded, but he disagreed with what Jonathan was saying. If his father couldn't see through her actions that Mary Margaret Westmoreland certainly wanted nothing to do with him, then Charlie would explain it in no uncertain terms. Under no circumstances would he ever give Mary Margaret another chance to become his wife, not after what she had just put him through.

"However," Jonathan continued, glancing in the direction where Meg had just disappeared, "that doesn't mean you can't have a little fun."

"Jonathan..." Charlie began.

"Hear me out," Jonathan interrupted. "She's a Third Class passenger. You couldn't possibly consider a relationship with her anyway. She's probably a mail order bride..."

"Really?"

"But, you deserve to live a little, too, you know? How many years has it been since you gave another woman a chance? For as long as I can remember you've been telling every beautiful woman that comes your way that you're engaged, and you can't even offer them a dance. Why not take a chance? She's beautiful—and if she's not married, why not?" Jonathan pressed.

"You know that's not how I operate anymore," Charlie reminded him, though the thought of pursuing Meg was very tempting. She was definitely one of the most beautiful women he had ever seen, if not the most beautiful. And despite momentarily misplacing her niece, she was also very good with children. She seemed warm and caring, and he could also see intelligence in her eyes.

"Let's just see if we run into sweet Meg again and play it by ear. What do you say?" Jonathan offered.

After a brief moment of pretended thoughtfulness, Charlie agreed. "All right," he said. "But really, what are the chances that I'll run into her again?"

"Right," Jonathan agreed, placing his hand on Charlie's shoulder as they began to head back to their own portion of the ship, "unless we continue to frequent the Third Class promenade."

"And the Squash Courts are also located below First Class accommodations," Charlie reminded him.

"And I hear they serve a mean cup of coffee in the Steerage Dining Hall," Jonathan laughed.

"Somehow I doubt that. Let's not push our luck," Charlie said. "If it's meant to be, it will work its way out."

"That's true," Jonathan agreed. "There's no way to escape one's destiny."

❧

"MUMMY!" Ruth yelled, rushing into her mother's arms just as soon as

Meg had the door open, despite the fact that Baby Lizzy was sleeping, as were her parents.

"Shhh!" Kelly scolded, still smiling at her little one as she flung her small body into her arms. "We mustn't be so loud when Baby Lizzy is asleep," she reminded.

"Sorry!" Ruth whispered sharply, almost as loudly as her normal volume. "Guess who I met!"

Meg took a deep breath and tossed herself onto her bunk. The furniture in the room was sparse, and there wasn't much space between the five occupants. Daniel was snoring on the top bunk above where Lizzy and Kelly were sleeping, and Ruth had the bunk above Meg. Though she had been tempted to ease back out the door, she knew this conversation was inevitable, and she may as well get it over with.

"Who did you meet?" Kelly asked as Ruth climbed into the crowded bed atop her mother.

"Uncle Charlie," she whispered, her hands on either side of her mouth. "And he helped me look for dawfins. We didn't see any, though."

Kelly looked from Ruth to Meg, puzzled. Meg was staring at the underside of the top bunk again, avoiding eye contact. "Uncle Charlie?" Kelly repeated. "Who is Uncle Charlie?"

"I told you," Ruth sighed over-dramatically. "He is my friend. We looked for dawfins. Then, Aunt Meg came, and he gave me back."

"What's that?" Kelly asked, clearly alarmed. "He gave you... back?"

"I'm sorry," Meg offered, rolling over to look at her friend, her head propped on her hand. "She just got away from me for a second. She's fine, though. She's perfectly fine."

Again, Kelly's eyes darted from Meg to Ruth and back again, finally coming to rest on her daughter's face. "Now, Ruthy," she began, taking her small hands in her larger ones, "you know how important it is never to run off, especially in a strange place. You could have gotten lost."

"Yes, Mummy," Ruth replied, her eyes downcast.

"What if this Charlie person had been a bad man? What if he would have hurt you?"

"No, Mummy, he isn't," Ruth insisted.

"How would you know?" Kelly questioned.

"I knew," Ruth replied. "As soon as I saw Uncle Charlie, I knew he was kind. And he is, Mummy. You'll see."

"And why are you calling this man you just met Uncle Charlie?" Kelly inquired.

Ruth shrugged and then leaned over to rest her head on her mother's neck, suddenly very tired from her excursions. "I'm sorry I scared you, Mummy. I love you."

"I love you, too, my angel," Kelly assured her, lovingly stroking her hair. "If anything ever happened to you, I don't know what I'd do. You and Lizzy are my everything."

Meg felt a tear trickling down her face. "I'm so sorry, Kelly," she whispered, knowing Ruth was falling asleep.

Kelly offered a smile, which Meg realized meant she was forgiven, even though the fear of speaking and waking slumbering children prevented the words from being said. Nevertheless, Meg vowed to make sure that Kelly's daughters were always safe. As long as she was breathing, she would protect those girls.

CHAPTER 4

"**A**re you absolutely certain?" Kelly asked as she and Meg sat on a bench near the Third Class Dining Hall.

"I think I would know," Meg assured her. Third Class dining was nothing like the events she was used to, and she could only imagine what Charlie and the rest of the socialites were preparing for in First Class aboard such a majestic vessel. Though dinner would start promptly at six o'clock, First Class dinners could last for hours, whereas Third Class could dine early and return to their chambers with sleeping children, as Daniel had, or stroll around the deck, as several other families were doing now. First Class diners would be up half the night pretending to be well-versed on topics of the day in order to impress each other. Though some Third Class passengers might be up partying until the wee hours of the morning, most of them would be asleep early, used to long days of hard work.

"But why would Charles Ashton be on the Third Class promenade? And of all people, why would my daughter run to him?" Kelly continued.

Meg shook her head. "I don't know, Kelly," she replied. "But I saw him two days ago outside of my house. I know what he looks like. And, unlike my mother, his parents constantly sent updated photographs.

I'm quite certain it was him—especially since he told both of us his name is Charlie."

Kelly continued to play devil's advocate. "You saw him out your bedroom window, two floors up, peering through drawn shades."

"He looked right at me," Meg insisted. "I'd recognize those eyes anywhere. Even though he couldn't see me, I certainly saw him."

"But he didn't recognize you?" Kelly clarified.

"No," Meg stated, pulling the shawl she had borrowed from Kelly tighter around her shoulders. Though she wasn't quite used to wearing these less restrictive clothes, she was very happy not to be completely cinched up in a tight corset and a formal gown.

Kelly continued to shake her head in disbelief. "It's all so peculiar," she said. "Did he ask your name?"

"No," Meg replied. "But his valet did. At least I think he was his valet. He said he was his friend. Anyway, no, Charlie didn't ask." She was temporarily distracted by the memory of that inquisitive expression Jonathan had plastered on his face, one that made her feel as if he was somehow on to her little charade.

"But what did you say when this other fellow asked?"

"Ruth answered for me," Meg explained. "She said I was 'Aunty Meg,' and then we walked away."

"Do you think he'll put two and two together?" Kelly inquired.

Meg had been pondering that same question for hours. Ultimately, however, did it really matter? "I'm not sure," she admitted. "But I don't think so. The thing is, if he didn't recognize me when I was standing right in front of him, that means the photographs he's received of me are so old, I no longer look like Mary Margaret Westmoreland to him. So, he would never suspect that I'm me. And he has no reason to think that a Third Class Steerage passenger would be me anyway. Does that make sense?"

"Yes, although you're not explaining it well," Kelly chided.

Meg gave her a slight shove. "Chances are I won't run into him again. I'm more worried that other First Class passengers, ones that have seen me at social events more regularly and recently, might recognize me. Those are the passengers I need to be leeriest of."

"Such as Lady Duff Gordon?" Kelly asked.

"Precisely, as well as the Strauses. They knew Father through the industry for a long time, and I'm fairly certain they would recognize me. As would Madeline Astor, for certain."

Kelly nodded. "All right. That shouldn't be too much of a problem. It's not like you'll be attending dinner in the First Class Banquet Hall."

"Heavens no," Meg agreed. "That is certainly not going to happen."

"With any luck, we'll arrive in New York without seeing Uncle Charlie again, as well," Kelly added.

"Yes," Meg nodded. "We'd be very lucky never to see Charles Ashton again." If only her heart agreed with the words coming out of her mouth. Despite everything, actually meeting Charlie in person had raised questions she had never even considered before. What if her parents really did know best? What if everything she had been fighting against for all of these years really was how her life was supposed to be? Meg pushed those thoughts aside. It didn't matter anymore. Her mother and her uncle had ruined any chances she had ever had of being a proper wife. The choices she had made after that may have cemented the damage they had already done, but it had begun there. And she knew she truly couldn't blame herself for their sins, though every time she closed her eyes that is precisely what she did. Ultimately, she didn't deserve Charles Ashton, and she knew it. It may have taken him a bit longer to figure it out, but the fact that he was here, and not in a Southampton hotel room waiting for her to reappear, assured her that he had drawn the same conclusion. He was certainly better off without her in his life.

"Why if it isn't Mr. Charles Ashton. Whatever are you doing here, darlin'? I thought you was planning on sticking around in Southampton for a while," an older, well-dressed woman asked as Charlie entered the First Class Dining Hall. He recognized her, of course, as millionaire Molly Brown from Colorado. He wasn't too surprised that she would find a way to make a prying question sound innocent enough.

"Mrs. Brown," he replied, "it's nice to see you. It seems I had a change of plans and am now available to join all of you on what is sure to be an historic maiden voyage of the RMS *Titanic*."

"Well, it sure is nice to see you as well," she gushed, not letting him get by so easily. "Where is your lovely betrothed, Miss Westmoreland? I would love to meet the young lady in person."

Charlie hesitated, staring into her eyes for a moment to ascertain whether or not she already knew the answer to that question. Since the inquiry seemed to be sincere, he determined she had no idea what had transpired between himself and Miss Westmoreland just a few days ago. "I believe Miss Westmoreland will be staying on in Southampton with her mother—for now."

If she had further questions, the appearance of Benjamin Guggenheim and his mistress, Leontine Aubert, was enough to draw her attention away from him at least long enough for him to make his escape. Charlie was never a big fan of these sorts of situations, and since Jonathan could not accompany him here, he was even more uncomfortable walking into a virtual wasps' nest all alone. He had managed to avoid this situation the night before because many of the First Class passengers had chosen to take dinner in their quarters, as had he, and the expectations of appearing on the first night of a voyage was lessened. However, there was simply no way to avoid this event two nights in a row without raising even more suspicion, so here he was, facing the fire as it were.

Luckily, he was seated at a table consisting almost exclusively of older couples, and very few of them were at all knowledgeable about his personal life or his engagement to Mary Margaret Westmoreland. Many of them knew his father and spoke only of his business. When he mentioned he was starting a company of his own, they were intrigued and asked several questions, which gave him many other things to talk about well off the topic of Miss Westmoreland. Molly Brown, who happened to be sitting across from him, was the only one who seemed to care at all about the suspicious circumstances surrounding his presence. Dinner was almost over before she asked, "So why'd you head back home so fast, stretch?"

Charlie considered the question as he took an overwhelmingly long time to choose the correct dessert fork before he finally said, "Timing is everything, isn't it, Mrs. Brown?"

Despite the fact that Molly Brown was outcast by many of the socialites because she was "new money," and therefore not considered worthy of their companionship, there was a knowing wisdom in her eyes, and Charlie realized he hadn't given her the veneration she deserved. After a few moments she simply said, "You're a good man, Charles Ashton. Don't let anyone tell you otherwise."

Charlie could feel the color creeping into his face, but he smiled at the woman across from him, saying quietly, "Thank you, and please, call me Charlie."

"Just so long as you call me Molly," she grinned, digging into her dessert.

When dinner was over, Charlie excused himself, intending to make a break for it before he could even be invited into the men's Smoking Lounge, but just before he reached the grand staircase and possible escape, J. J. Astor stepped in front of him, offering him his hand. "Charlie," he said in quick recognition. "I had heard you were aboard the *Titanic*, though we weren't expecting you. What a pleasant surprise. How are you?"

"I'm well, thank you, sir. And yourself?" he replied, forcing a smile and taking the older gentleman's hand.

"We are doing quite well," Astor assured him just as his wife, Madeline, joined him, slipping her arm through his. "I don't believe you've met my wife. This is Madeline." The diminutive woman offered him her hand, which he took as her husband introduced him.

Upon hearing his name, Madeline gave a nod of recognition. "Yes, of course, Charlie. It's nice to meet you at last," she smiled. As she began to glance around with a curious expression on her face, Charlie braced himself for the inevitable question. "Where is..."

"Miss Westmoreland is not accompanying me back to New York," he interrupted before she could even finish the question.

"Oh," Madeline replied, still puzzled. "That's too bad. I should have liked to have seen her. It's been a few years since we have had the chance to speak."

Charlie realized that, despite Mr. Astor's age, Madeline was younger than him, and possibly younger than Mary Margaret as well. And she was also quite obviously pregnant. Not sure of exactly what one was to say under these circumstances, and knowing they were also on their honeymoon, he simply said, "I suppose congratulations are in order," with a smile.

"Oh, yes, thank you," she replied, returning his smile and running a hand across her abdomen. "It won't be too much longer now."

"Charlie, if you'll excuse us, I will be escorting Mrs. Astor back to our chambers before I join the rest of the gentlemen in the lounge. You will be joining us, won't you?" J.J. asked, the expression on his face implying Charlie should do so.

Despite what could only be ascertained as insistence by arguably one of the richest men in the world, Charlie declined. "I'm afraid I won't be able to this evening, Mr. Astor."

"Please, call me J.J.," he said, dismissively. "Why not? You'll miss out on all of the important discussions," he continued, a twinkle in his eye that showed he knew most of what was said in such situations was of little value.

Charlie smiled politely. "I'm afraid I have some business matters to attend to myself." He hoped his excuse would stick, and as Mr. Astor nodded in understanding, he began to think he would be able to retreat successfully after all.

"Very well then. But tomorrow night! I'm holding you to it!" J. J. Astor insisted.

"Tomorrow night it is," Charlie assured him, taking his offered hand one more time. "It was a pleasure to meet you, Mrs. Astor," he added.

"You as well," she replied. As her husband began to lead her out of the room, she turned and over her shoulder called, "Oh, and when you see her, tell Meg I said hello."

Charlie paused mid-step and turned back to look at her, not sure he had heard correctly. "What was that?" he asked.

She had stopped now, seeing the confused expression on his face. "Meg," she repeated, "Mary Margaret. When you see her, please tell her I said hello."

"Right, yes, of course," Charlie said, nodding his head. Once again, he turned and resumed his ascension up the staircase. *How odd*, he thought. *In all of the years that I've known Mary Margaret, I've never heard anyone call her Meg. Now, today, on the day that I meet a beautiful woman named Meg, someone refers to this woman I've been engaged to for three years by the exact same nickname. What a strange coincidence.*

CHAPTER 5

B
y the time he reached his cabin, the peculiar thought had almost left him completely. He knew Jonathan wouldn't expect him back for several hours, assuming he would not be able to escape the lounge. He poured himself a brandy and made his way out to the private deck. The evening was chilly, but the air felt good, and he was hoping it would clear his mind. While visions of little Ruth and her intriguing aunt were welcome thoughts, his mind kept returning to the events of the last few days that had led him to his current position. It all seemed a bit surreal, but then so had his entire engagement, quite honestly, and only now that it seemed to be over did he feel he could finally get on with his life at long last.

He had arrived in London to attend to a few business matters, both on behalf of his father's steel company as well as the new celluloid manufacturing company he was starting on his own. His father had made a name for himself in the steel industry early on, amassing a fortune on wise business decisions, and while Charlie certainly intended to continue working in his father's business, he felt that there was also a fortune to be made in celluloid compound manufacturing, particularly for packaging purposes. Of course, once he married Mary Margaret, he would also take over her father's textile company, something he truly wasn't interested in, but he knew how important it was to his father to ensure Henry Westmoreland's legacy lived on.

At least that is one less concern, he thought as he peered out across the pristine surface of the Atlantic. His understanding was that the Westmoreland company was not doing well under the inept eye of her uncle, Bertram Westmoreland, a drunkard and womanizer from all accounts, and Charlie wasn't even certain it was salvageable. But he had certainly intended to do his best. He knew his father had made promises to Henry before his death—several of them. Exactly why, he did not know, but if his father intended for him to salvage the business and marry the daughter, then that is precisely what he intended to do.

That all changed when he showed up in Southampton on April 7 expecting to meet Mary Margaret Westmoreland for the first time at the debutant ball of a mutual friend only to be told Miss Westmoreland would not be attending. When he called at her home the next day, he was told by her mother that she was not feeling well and that he should call again on the ninth. Upon his return, she informed him that her daughter had been kidnapped and that she had reported her missing to the police. By then, however, rumors had begun to circulate, reaching the careful ear of his assistant, and the possibility that Miss Westmoreland had actually disappeared with one of the household servants became the most likely explanation for why she had not been available these past three times he had come to call on her. He was certain that, if this were the case, Mrs. Westmoreland was aware that her daughter had actually eloped with this jack-of-all-trades, the son of a long-time house servant, and that she was simply reporting her daughter's absence as a kidnapping in order to buy time and save face.

The next morning, he had booked his passage and set sail on the *Titanic*.

"Well, wherever you are, Mary Margaret, I hope you are happy with the path that you've chosen," he mumbled as he finished his drink and slammed the glass down on the railing, not caring if it fell overboard or not. A rapping on the door caught his attention. He was certain that Jonathan would have simply let himself in. Curious as to whom might be calling on him at this hour, he made his way across the room to the door.

"You awake, Charlie?" Molly Brown asked, barely giving him time to open the door before she invited herself in. "Been thinkin' about you and wanted to see how you was doin'."

Charlie glanced out into the hallway before closing the door behind her, wondering if anyone had just seen an un-chaperoned female enter his private chambers. Though Mrs. Brown was older, she was divorced, and the last thing he needed was more fodder for the rumor mongers.

"Don't worry," she said, as if reading his mind. "Nobody knows I'm here." She poured herself a drink and had a seat on his sofa. "Can you imagine? If people want to talk about the two of us, that's fine by me. Handsome young feller like you with me? I'm old enough to be your mama, son. Now, what's this business I hear with you and this Westmoreland gal?"

Once again, Charlie found himself glancing around in confusion. He realized he needed another drink. Since his original glass was probably somewhere in Davey Jones's locker, he grabbed a new one and poured four fingers worth before sitting down in a chair across from her. "I'm not exactly sure how to answer that," Charlie replied after throwing back more of the sweet liquid than he initially intended. "I guess it depends on what you've heard."

"Oh, come on now, son," Molly pried. "Surely you know me well enough by now to know I ain't got a reserved bone in my body. After you lit out of dinner so quick, I asked some questions and found out Miss Mary Margaret's gone on the lam herself. She ain't on this boat, too somewhere, is she?"

"No," Charlie replied hastily. "Why would you say that?"

"Well, I was just wondering if you didn't decide to sneak off together and get hitched without all them prim and proper folks interferin'."

Charlie was stunned at that response as he never would have thought anyone would consider that possibility; it had never crossed his mind. "No, Mrs. Brown—Molly—I can assure you that I did not smuggle Miss Westmoreland aboard the *Titanic*. But whoever told you she is missing seems to have some inside knowledge. Her mother told me the same when I called on her just two days ago. In fact, I have never even met Miss Westmoreland. So, I think it is fair to say that whatever arrangements our fathers made are out the window." With that, he finished off the rest of his drink, realizing the alcohol was about to get to him and wondering if he even cared. Deciding he didn't, he stood, poured himself another drink, and topped Molly's off as well.

"Well, I do declare," she said after a few moments of contemplation. "I'd heard she may have run off with the missin' servants, but I didn't think that was likely. Whole thing seems so peculiar. Course everybody says she didn't get along with her mother at all, and that uncle of hers has quite the reputation. I wouldn't want to be alone with him—and I'm an old divorced bitty who doesn't generally take too much persuasion."

Molly spoke quickly with a thick western accent, and much of what she said raised several questions in Charlie's head. He sat staring at her until he was sure she had finished before contemplating where to begin. "I'm sorry, Molly. Did you say servants? As in more than one?"

"Sure did," she confirmed, taking another swig. "One of the house boys is gone, and so is Miss Mary's lady. Makes sense she'd go wherever her mistress has gone. But she had a family. Whole bunch is missing. Odd."

"That is odd," Charlie agreed, although he moved on before she began to talk again and lost him. "And what did you say about her uncle?"

"Bertram Westmoreland is not the kind of man anyone wants to be left alone with, especially not young impressionable girls," she explained. "Now, I don't know about his own niece, but the man has a reputation for being pretty handsy."

Charlie nodded. He had heard that before, but considering Mary Margaret was engaged to be his wife, and she was Bertram's family, he never thought she was at any risk. The uncle had lived with Mary Margaret's parents even before she was born. The older brother of Henry by a considerable margin, he had wasted away his portion of the family inheritance before Henry even graduated from university, and by the time the younger brother began his textile company, Bertram was eagerly awaiting any opportunity to profit from his brother's hard work. Charlie had met him a few times when he had come to New

York on business, and though he had been frightening as a young child, he seemed like a harmless old man now. Molly seemed to think otherwise. "Do you think something shady was going on?"

"I'm not sure," Molly replied, finishing her drink. "I know one of the girls was saying Bertram wouldn't take no for an answer once several years back at a coming out party... ball, what have you... and if her now-husband hadn't happened by at just the right moment, she was fairly certain he'd have his way with her one way or another."

As Charlie sat contemplating this new information, wondering precisely what had become of Mary Margaret after all, Jonathan let himself in. At first, he looked confused, but it took only a moment for Molly to jump up, grab him by the hand and introduce herself, as if they were equals. "Molly just stopped by to speak to me about Miss Westmoreland," Charlie explained as Jonathan refilled his glass without being asked.

"I see," he replied, sitting the decanter back down. "So word has reached our vessel at sea, then?"

"Have a seat, pumpkin," Molly said, gesturing at the spot next to her on the couch. "Southampton society ain't much different than New York. People got somethin' to talk about, they're gonna talk."

"And what are they saying?" he inquired, taking the seat he was offered and glancing from one face to the other.

"For the most part, nothing we haven't heard," Charlie replied. "Except for the fact that I didn't realize her lady-in-waiting and her family had also gone with her."

Jonathan nodded, as if this was not new information to him after all. "And I'm sure you know by now, then, that people are assuming they are all here with you?"

Charlie raised an eyebrow. "Yes," he confirmed. "And you've known this since...."

"Well, there was no point in mentioning it. After all, it's obviously not true," he explained.

"But if I had known, it might have saved a little embarrassment at dinner," Charlie countered.

"Would you have done anything differently?" Jonathan shot back.

Again, Charlie considered the question. "No, I suppose not."

"Best to just let them think whatever they want, then," Molly offered. "Right now, they're assumin' she's aboard, all them servants are, too, and the rumor that she was sleepin' with the house boy is just fiddle faddle."

"I'm sorry—what?" Charlie asked, almost dropping his glass. "I know it had been mentioned that there was speculation they may have eloped, but no one ever said...."

"Oh, bless your poor innocent heart," Molly said. "Sorry darlin'. I just figured you knew one meant the other."

Charlie was up now and pacing the small area in front of the chair. "Is that true? Do you think that's true? This whole time, I've been refusing to dance with other women at balls, hardly opened a door... I once told a woman I couldn't help her out of a motor coach because I was engaged.... Surely she hasn't been.... The entire time...."

"Charlie, boy, settle down, now," Molly insisted, standing and taking him gently by the arms and pushing him back into the chair. "Nobody knows, and ain't nobody gonna know, till Miss Sunshine shows up and tells her story. Till then, why don't you go have some fun? Find some pretty girls and ask them to dance. Hell, I hear there's a motor coach downstairs. Take it for a spin. You've got to relax a little, son. Right now, you're wound up tighter than an eight-day clock."

"Mrs. Brown, I think perhaps Charlie needs to get some rest," Jonathan began taking a step toward the door.

"He needs to go to bed all right, but I ain't sure it's for sleep," she muttered. "You stop blamin' yourself for this mess, Charlie. You have no idea what was goin' on across the ocean, halfway around the world, you hear me?"

Charlie was sitting in the chair, his elbows on his knees, his head resting on his interlaced fingers, only partially listening to what Mrs. Brown had to say. He wasn't sure if it was the alcohol or the ever increasing level of foolishness he had fallen victim to that made him feel suddenly very angry, but either way, he was doing his best to contain himself as Jonathan ushered Molly out of the room.

Once she was gone and the door was locked behind her, Jonathan sat back down on the edge of the couch, saying, "She's right. You can't take any of this personally."

"Can't take it personally? Jonathan, she was cheating on me! With a servant!"

"You don't know that," his friend reminded him. "But even if she was, as Mrs. Brown said, you don't know why she would do those things. She never even met you."

"You're right, she didn't. I wrote letter after letter, sent telegrams, cards. Pictures. Occasionally, if I was lucky, she would send something back. Some overly formal jibber jabber obviously proofread by her mother. Nothing personal, nothing intimate. Ever. In three years. Longer, really, if you consider all of that pre-engagement nonsense. That whole time, I was trying to do what my father asked me to do, and she was over there, doing... him." He was exhausted by that point, both physically and mentally. He pressed himself back against the chair, doing his best to hold it together.

"Let's get some sleep," Jonathan said calmly, "and reevaluate the situation in the morning. Clearly, we aren't going to have much new information so long as we are on a boat in the middle of the ocean. But once we get back to New York, we can try contacting Mrs. Westmoreland and see if she has any word as to where Mary Margaret might be and if she can tell us any more information about this servant of theirs."

Charlie nodded in agreement and hauled himself up out of the chair. Perhaps tomorrow would bring new perspective, but as for now, sleep was the only possible escape from this ever-growing circle of deception. Moments later, when his head hit the pillow, he was determined to push the demons aside and try to focus on the angelic face of the blonde-haired woman he'd met earlier that day. Perhaps she was the secret to ending all of this ridicule and tomfoolery.

HER BEDROOM WAS ALWAYS DARK. She wanted the shades open, at least partially, so some of the light from the street, or better still, the stars, could shine in. But no matter how many times she opened them, even if it was just a crack, her mother's lady, Ms. Julia, would always come in just as she was about to drift off and close them. Even when she had asked nicely, even when she had begged her mother, she was told they needed to be closed. Closed tight.

It was the same nearly every night. She'd beg to stay up, to read another book, to sit by the fire, even to clean her room. Eventually, her mother would have enough and send her up. She'd linger with the toiletries, sometimes insisting on putting on several of her nightshirts all at the same time. In the summer it was unbearable to do so, but then, so was the alternative. Of course, it didn't make a difference. Regardless of what she wore, it never made a difference.

Eventually, she'd give in and nod off to restless sleep for a few hours —waiting, always waiting. She hadn't slept fully in years, not since she was a small girl. Not since her father died. It wasn't too long after his death that the horror began. Just about the time her body began to relax, the tension in her shoulders unclenching, there would be a creak in the hallway, the turn of a key, and she would begin to weep.

At first, it was scary and uncomfortable, but then it became extremely painful, and as spindly fingers probed deeper and harder, it was almost too much for her little body to bear. If she cried too loudly, he would shove a pillow against her face, threatening to smother her; sometimes, she wanted him to. He always said what he was doing wasn't wrong, that he wasn't ruining her for her husband, that he didn't push hard enough to do so. He said blood was bad. Only if there was blood would she be spoilt. And then, one day when she was ten, she woke up to bloody sheets. She had cried even harder that day, knowing already of her father's promise, that she was damaged now and could never truly fulfill his wishes, never be the wife he had meant for her to be. When she was twelve, she gathered the courage to tell her mother and was greeted with a slap in the face so hard it jarred her teeth. Shortly thereafter, she realized her doorway was not the only one he was darkening, and any implications on her part meant her mother was not all the woman she should be.

When she was about fourteen, the visits became less frequent for a while. She noticed her mother began employing women with young daughters, some no more than six. Her heart hurt for these little girls. She attempted to speak to their mothers, but they needed employment, and her pleas fell on deaf ears. It seemed no matter who she spoke to, no one wanted to listen, no one except for Kelly. She had been there to hold her through the worst of it, to wipe away her tears. She had even faced her mother once. A broken nose for the lady-in-waiting and a visit from her uncle later, Meg had insisted that Kelly never say another word to anyone. She said if she did, she would deny it. And Kelly complied.

Once the engagement was official, her uncle began to remind her quite frequently again whom she really belonged to. Fearful that she would put Kelly in harm's way again, she assured her friend that he had stopped, that his attention was focused elsewhere. It was then that she had turned to Ezra. She had found her solace in the charming servant boy who often made household repairs and worked in the coach house. And whenever Kelly caught her crying, she would simply say she was having nightmares. Because that was true. And even aboard the *Titanic*, the nightmares didn't stop.

On the night of April 11, the morning of the twelfth, Meg awoke in a cold sweat, realizing she was panting, hoping her thrashing about had not been so loud as to wake the sleeping children. Despite the realness of her terrifying dream, she realized everyone else was still fast asleep. She attempted to push the memories of the nightmare from her mind, but it had been so vivid, it was almost impossible. This dream had been so similar to all of the others, but the ending had been vastly different. In the end, she was sinking, plunged beneath frigid water, a hand pulling her down to the ocean floor. She caught just a glimpse of that hand before she forced herself awake. She recognized those spindly fingers oh so well.

Pulling herself to the edge of her bed, she carefully swung herself out from under the top bunk and pulled on her robe. She wouldn't go far, but she needed some air. All of the clothing she had with her was borrowed save this one pink bathrobe her mother had given her for her birthday last year. It was the only item she was certain no one from First Class could possibly see, and she wasn't about to let them see it now. Still, she needed to breathe.

She wasn't sure how safe it was to be out in the middle of the night all by herself, but at that point, she felt there was very little else anyone could take from her. Gazing down into the same depths she had just drowned in, she realized this dream was a metaphor for her life. Her uncle had taken everything from her. He had set in motion a chain reaction that led to her destruction. She had made some irresponsible choices along the way, too, no doubt. But ultimately, the demise of Mary Margaret Westmoreland began when Bertram Westmoreland started to pull her deeper and deeper below the surface, forcing the life from her, creating a situation where she could no longer fulfill the destiny she was meant to.

She glanced up at the star filled sky, realizing for the first time that Charlie was just as much a victim in this as she was. For the longest time, she had taken out her anger and frustration on him because he was an easy target. After all, she'd never even met him, yet she was being forced to marry him. How dare he even pretend to care for her, to insinuate he was willingly complying with his father's wishes? He was arguably the most eligible bachelor in New York City. Why would he agree to marry her—an Englishwoman he'd never even met, one with hardly a few pence to her name and only a washed up textile business to offer?

She had thought at first, perhaps, he was after that. Maybe he thought this was his only opportunity to make his own name for himself. But then he had begun to write to her about other interests he was pursuing, other industries. He mentioned celluloid, for example, and something about petroleum. So, his willingness to comply had nothing to do with opportunity.

Then she thought perhaps he was hideously ugly, and the pictures he sent were of someone else. But she'd seen him in the newspapers and knew he was strikingly handsome, perhaps the most dashing man she'd ever laid eyes on. The fact that he could have any number of other girls but chose to have her made her even angrier, to the point that she just assumed surely he was having those other girls, though he wrote to her constantly of his devotion to her and to her alone.

She wondered if, perhaps, he was quite dull-witted. Perhaps someone else wrote the letters he sent to her. But she knew that would not escape mention in the local gossip rings. No, there was absolutely nothing wrong with Charles J. Ashton. Nothing at all. He was absolutely perfect, and she was not. And she had hated him for it.

Which made it even easier to do what she had done. She took every opportunity available to avoid him. She delayed and denied. And the night of her friend Alise's coming out ball, she did the worst thing imaginable. It was the only thing she could think of, one last ditch effort to escape Charles Ashton at last.

And, to some extent, it had worked. After all, she was no longer to be his wife.

But staring into the abyss beneath her, Meg was certain she had made a horrible mistake. And she could not undo any of the things she had done. Now, she realized, the best thing for her to do was to quietly slip out of existence. And that is why she had decided to go ahead with her plan, even without Ezra. Even after Kelly had come into her room that terrible morning just two days ago with those awful, awful words dripping from her tongue.

"He's gone."

When she returned to the cabin, she slipped in as quietly as possible, disrobed, and climbed back into bed, hoping she had not disturbed anyone. However, a few moments later, Kelly unwound herself from Baby Lizzy and slid in beside her, wrapping her arm beneath her shoulders. "Everythin' okay, darlin'?" she whispered.

"Yes," Meg replied as quietly as possible. "I just had another bad dream, that's all."

"I'm so sorry," her friend replied, kissing her gently on the forehead. "It'll get better, the farther away from England we go. You'll see."

Meg nodded. "I hope so. I just... I keep thinking about Charlie, too, and how lucky he is that, despite the ridicule he may be suffering now, how things are so much better now that I am out of his life forever. He didn't deserve to be married to someone like me... someone who's capable of the things I've done."

"Meg!" Kelly scolded. "How can you say something like that? The things your uncle did to you were not your fault. You can't possibly hold yourself responsible for his transgressions."

"Maybe not, but the choices I made after that were all my own. For the longest time, I didn't understand how Charlie could be so readily acceptable of someone else's plan for his life. After meeting him today, I realized, that's just who he is. He wanted to do what his father asked him to do while I rebelled against it. Then, I did everything I could to spite my mother, ultimately leaving Charlie and his feelings in my wake. I would like to say I never meant to hurt him, but I know that's not true. Charlie wasn't just a circumstantial casualty in this—my actions that damaged his reputation and potentially broke his heart were calculated on my part, and that's something I am very much ashamed of."

"Meg, I don't think that's completely true. I've been with you through all of this, remember? While I know you chose to skip out on Alise's ball purposefully, knowing Charlie would be waiting for you, I honestly believe that was only because you knew it would have the deepest impact on your mother—which it did—not because of Charlie directly."

Meg shook her head. "Maybe. I don't know. I just... I've had a lot of bitterness toward him, and it's been unwarranted. I wish there was some way I could make it up to him, could apologize. But any attempt at doing so would make it far worse. It's best for me—for Mary Margaret Westmoreland—to stay out of his life forever. So, if we run into him again whilst aboard this ship, you must promise to help me avoid him, all right?"

Kelly considered the statement before replying. Finally, she said, "Meg, are you sure you shouldn't take advantage of this opportunity to talk to him, to clear the air? You're right—he does seem like an honorable chap. Perhaps if you approached him and explained everything—and I mean everything—he could at least have some peace about the situation, knowing he didn't do anything wrong."

"You can't be serious!" Meg exclaimed, causing Baby Lizzy to stir in the bed across from them. "Sorry," she muttered in a sharp whisper. "I didn't mean to... but no. I couldn't possibly.... He'd never understand anyway."

After glancing over at her daughter to make sure she was still asleep, Kelly returned her attention to her friend. "Perhaps you aren't giving the gentleman enough credit, Meg. I'm sure that, if you told him what your uncle did, he'd understand. Maybe you don't have to tell him about Ezra, but letting him know you're sorry would be a step in the right direction toward mending both of your wounded hearts."

Meg shook her head adamantly. "Absolutely not," she replied. "Under no circumstances will I ever attempt to explain my poor decision making to Charles Ashton, nor will I attempt to explain it away through playing the victim. Please don't attempt to necessitate such a meeting either, Kelly. I just want to leave him be, let him live his life, and pray that someday I'll find someone who's willing to accept me, despite my flaws."

Again, Kelly considered her statement before finally resting her head on Meg's shoulder and saying, "Fine, I won't press the issue, but I think you'd feel much better if you'd get it off of your chest. And someday you will find a man who loves you just as much as you deserve to be loved, my darlin'. I wish you could see yourself as I see you. You are an amazing person, Meggy, and I hate that you've lost yourself through all of this. Someday you'll see yourself for who you really are again."

"Thank you, love," Meg said, kissing her dearest on the top of her head before Kelly crossed back over to cradle her babe. Meg turned to face the whitewashed wall, Kelly's words replaying in her mind. If only what she said were true. But Meg knew in her heart she would never be worthy of the kind of love Kelly and Daniel had, the kind that Charlie had promised her at one point in their engagement. At the time, she had laughed it off, sure he was only making promises he never intended to keep. Now, she realized she had given up so much more than she had ever realized all in the name of revenge.

The saddest part about the entire situation was that, while she was certain her mother was at home mourning her loss, it was the forfeiture of her chances at gaining position that would have her distraught, not the absence of her daughter. She had lost any semblance of care for her only living child long ago.

With a few hours until sunrise, Meg attempted to fall back to sleep, praying that this time the nightmares would stay away and she could get some much needed rest at last.

CHAPTER 6

J onathan Lane was a wiz at gaining information, in any situation, in any location, and being aboard the *Titanic* had not limited his resourcefulness. Though they had just encountered little Ruth and her Aunty Meg the day before, he had already ascertained a room number, the names of Ruth's parents—Daniel and Kelly O'Connell—and the fact that the other woman sharing their room was registered on the ship's roster as Meg Sister, which he thought was rather odd and perhaps a clerical mistake. Early on the morning of April 12, he ran into a steward for Steerage passengers who mentioned the peculiar sight of a very attractive, fair-haired passenger leaving Third Class accommodations dressed in a pink robe in the middle of the night, spending several minutes peering into the Atlantic before returning to her cabin. He said the only thing truly unusual about it was the fact that the robe did not match the class. It seemed rather expensive, he noted.

Jonathan wasn't sure if this was important information or not, but he filed it away for later use. Even if Third Class passenger Meg Sister, or Aunty Meg as it were, was only meant as a bit of fun, there was always the possibility she may attempt to take advantage of the current emotional state of the charming millionaire, and it was up to Jonathan to make sure that the situation improved, that nothing happened to worsen Charlie's disposition.

Charlie had awoken with a bit of a headache and some churning in his stomach he could not attribute to the movement of the boat. Rather, it was the liquor that had caused these unwelcome symptoms. Despite feeling a bit under the weather, the new day shed some fresh light on his situation. Standing on his deck, sipping black coffee, gazing out at the sunrise, he was determined to no longer allow Mary Margaret Westmoreland control of his destiny. He had done so for far too long. Likewise, he resolved not to care what other members of his social class may have to say about his personal situation. It was none of their business. If they wanted to make speculations as to what went wrong between himself and his betrothed, they were entitled to think whatever they wanted. Their opinions of him were, frankly, of little concern. If Miss Westmoreland had obtained a reputation as a two-bit hussy, well, there was not much he could do to repair that either. He just hoped, for her own sake, whatever had gone awry was on the up and up, and she could live with the decision she had made.

With little coaxing from Jonathan, he had dressed and joined several of his acquaintances in the dining hall for breakfast. While it was evident some whispering was going on behind gloved hands, he paid little attention. Those who chose to talk about him would do so whether there was new information or not. He and Jonathan sat with Benjamin Guggenheim and his valet, Victor Giglio. Mr. Guggenheim had provided recent fodder for the rumor mills himself, showing up on the steamship with his mistress rather than his wife, so honestly, at times it was hard to tell if the prying eyes were directed at him or the senior gentlemen.

Guggenheim's relationship with his valet was very similar to Charlie's with Jonathan. Rather than just a working relationship, Benjamin and Victor were actually very good friends, as was evident by the conversation that passed between them. Guggenheim discussed several pieces of art he had recently acquired as well as some business information, but his main topic of dialogue was his philanthropic efforts with the poor of New York, and Charlie began to realize that Mr. Guggenheim was certainly more than an astute businessman; he was also a champion for the underprivileged, something he had not previously realized.

"If we can't help other people along on this journey, then I say, what is the purpose, you know, Ashton? That's my sentiment anyway," Guggenheim waxed after breakfast was over. "They're going to talk about everything we do. We may as well stun them and do something extraordinarily benevolent," he continued. "I've got plans in the works, you see. Big plans to start a charity organization that will change the way every child in New York City is educated."

"That sounds very interesting," Charlie admitted. "What do you propose?"

"Well, I haven't quite got it all sorted out yet, but it will revolutionize the way the poor are educated. You just wait and see," Guggenheim continued, already nursing a brandy at just shy of nine o'clock in the morning.

Charlie was sticking with coffee, black, hoping the ringing in his ears would dissipate. "Well, keep me abreast of any new developments. I'd like to be involved," he offered.

"Will do, Charlie my boy," Guggenheim laughed. "Will do. I'm sure you could offer some insight. Now, if you don't mind the advice of an experienced gentlemen of these circles, let me give you my two cents about the whispering scandalizers amongst us: do whatever you can to confuse them. It's much more fun to jump in with both feet just to see what you can stir up than it is to let their speculation and dirty looks ruin your disposition. If they think this girl is hidden on the boat somewhere, show up with an unidentified woman who looks similar. If they think she ran off with the footmen, show up with a nursemaid. You can't let them dictate to you what you should or should not do. Likewise, if this Westmoreland girl really did decide some common John was better for her than you, I say good riddance. There are plenty of other young socialites on the scene, old chap. You may as well choose another to tie yourself to for the rest of your life, and then you're free to do as you please."

Charlie listened intently, eyes-wide, particularly to the last part. "Well, Mr. Guggenheim..."

"Ben, please..."

"Ben, I suppose I hadn't considered all of that. I appreciate your sentiment, although I have to say I had always imagined my marriage would be similar to that of my parents, solid and unwavering. I never imagined..."

"No one ever does, my boy. But very rarely does it ever turn out the way we think it will. And I'll tell you, I love my wife and my daughters in a way I cannot describe. But it's Leontine who keeps me sane."

With that, the gentlemen parted ways, wishing each other a fine day. As Jonathan and Charlie made their way out onto the adjoining deck, Jonathan said, "Well, that's the same advice from two very different, yet unusually similar, individuals. What do you say? Shall we make our way back to C Deck?"

"Lead the way," Charlie insisted, gesturing with his palm face up. Perhaps he should have started listening to the council of his peers a long time ago.

༺༻

RUTH HAD all but refused to eat a bite of her breakfast, insisting that they make their way to the deck as soon as possible so that she could continue her pursuit of finding "dawfins." However, the longer she fussed the more waiting she had to endure, and by the time they had finished at last, they had one cranky, persnickety little girl on their hands.

Meg followed behind the family, Ruth's small hands grasping her parents' as she led them to her favorite spot for dawfin watching, about where she had run into Charlie only the day before. Meg was holding a sleeping Lizzy, rocking her gently, and cooing at her softly. Even though Lizzy was not her own, she couldn't help but treat her as such in these small moments when she had the baby in her arms.

As Ruth turned around to tell Meg something, her face broke into a wide smile, and she immediately burst free from her parents' grasps, shouting, "Uncle Charlie!" as she shot past Meg down the promenade.

"Well, hello there, my little friend," Charlie said, scooping her up. Her parents followed closely behind, and the look of consternation on her mother's face was telling. "Now, Ruthy, what did your Aunty Meg tell you about darting off?"

Ruth frowned. "I'm sorry, Uncle Charlie. I didn't mean to run away. I was just so happy to see you."

"I understand, little lass, but you must stay with your parents. It's not safe to be running about on a ship with wet decks. You could fall. Or you could get lost," he replied, attempting to hand her back to her mother.

Ruth hung on tightly, wiggling her legs in protest. "No, Uncle Charlie. I want you to show me the dawfins," she insisted, pointing to the spot she had recently vacated.

Daniel shrugged and extended his hand to Charlie. "She seems to have latched on to you. I'm Daniel O'Connell," he said. "I heard you found her yesterday as well. Thank you for your kindness, Mr. Ashton. So sorry for the trouble."

"Oh, it's no trouble," Charlie insisted, crossing over to the railing where Ruth's wild gestures indicated she wanted to go. "Ruth and I are fast friends now, aren't we?" he said, smiling at the little girl.

She nodded. "And today we're going to see some real DAWFINS!" she exclaimed, peering off into the water.

"I hope so," Charlie laughed. "Mr. O'Connell, this is my friend Jonathan Lane," he continued, making the introduction as Daniel and Jonathan both insisted on first names. Glancing around, he finally made eye contact with Meg, and smiling around the back of Ruth's fiery head of hair, he said, "Hello, Aunty Meg. How are you this fine day?"

Meg blushed despite herself. She had intentionally hung back when she saw where Ruth was running, knowing the child was in no danger. She had hoped she could sneak away, but since she was still holding Lizzy, it seemed rather odd to do so. Now that she had an opportunity to address Kelly, she began to think of a quick exit strategy. However, those green eyes were locked on her, and the words seemed to be twisted around her tongue. Finally, she managed to say, "Good morning

Mr. Ashton—Charlie. Good morning, Jonathan. I'm well, thank you. And yourselves?"

Jonathan nodded, which she took to mean he was doing just fine, and Charlie replied, "Quite well, thank you. There's just something about the fresh air to brighten one's mood, don't you think?"

Meg found his comment rather peculiar, considering she knew more about his situation than she should, but she only smiled and nodded in agreement. "Well, if you'll excuse me, I'm going to lay sweet Lizzy down for a nap," she said, managing to pull her eyes away from his long enough to glance down at that precious baby face.

"Oh, I'd be happy to escort you," Charlie said, a look of disappointment on his face.

Though Ruth was already loudly protesting Charlie's departure, Meg assured him it wasn't necessary. "Thank you, but I can manage," she replied and then added. "Besides, I'd hate for you to miss any dawfins."

Charlie glanced back out to sea before returning his gaze to her. "I'm sure the dawfins will still be here when I return," he said.

Meg could tell by Kelly's expression that she was dying to say something, obviously thinking Meg should take advantage of the offer. A stern look from her former mistress was enough to remind her of their earlier conversation, and Meg repeated her declination. "I'll be just fine by myself, thank you."

"I'll walk with you," Jonathan offered. "That way we'll be sure you make it to the cabin without incident, and Uncle Charlie can stay to view any wayward dawfins."

There seemed to be some exchange of looks between the two gentlemen as well, and Kelly nodded at Meg, insisting she let Jonathan escort her. "Very well then, thank you," she acquiesced. "It was a pleasure to see you again, Mr. Ashton," she said cordially. "Ruth, mind your mummy, love," she reminded and then let Jonathan guide her toward the stairwell that would take them several decks below to where their cabin was located. Due to the late booking, they were given a room on one of the lower decks, and though it wasn't ideal, they had been happy just to have a room at all.

"How are you finding your accommodations?" Jonathan asked as they strolled along.

Meg considered her response carefully. Of course, to her, Third Class rooms were nothing like what she was used to. Yet, to someone of Aunty Meg's stature, they should be quite the upgrade from the holding cells one would expect. That is, if one had ever even been on an ocean liner before. Rather than try to determine exactly what he might be getting at—if anything—she simply said, "I can't complain," and smiled at him warmly.

"Good," Jonathan replied, returning the smile. "I've heard they are some of the best available when it comes to Steerage."

"We have enough room for everyone," she assured him. There were several other people about, but all of them were also Third Class passengers, and everyone smiled and nodded in greeting, clearly enjoying their third day on the voyage.

There was a momentary pause, and Meg wondered if he was giving her an opportunity to speak. Though she could hardly bear the awkward silence, she was determined to say as few words as possible. The less she said, the less the chances of slipping up and saying something only Mary Margaret Westmoreland could know.

It seemed Jonathan didn't like the lack of conversation either. Eventually, he asked, "What are your plans once you reach America, Miss Meg?"

"Oh, I'm not sure yet," she admitted. They had made their way to the stairwell, and she was ever so cautious to watch her footing above the sleeping babe's head as she made her descent. Jonathan seemed ready, lest she slip or fall, but she made it safely down, heading toward the corridor.

Once she reached level ground, he asked, "What was your trade in England?"

"Actually," she dodged, "America is all about fresh starts. I think I may try my hand at something entirely different than what I am used to." She could see their room just at the end of the hall, and though she didn't mind Jonathan's questions, they were becoming more personal and more pointed.

"That sounds like an exciting venture," he replied. "And what does Mr. O'Connell do?"

"He's a carpenter," Meg replied quickly, without stopping to wonder if doing so could be problematic.

"I see. And Mrs. O'Connell—your sister?"

Meg smiled. "Clearly, you can see we are not actually sisters."

"No, of course not," he replied. "Just friends then?"

"Precisely," she nodded. "Life-long friends. We may as well be sisters." She couldn't help but wonder if she had just been given a test of some sort, as if Jonathan was trying to ascertain if she would lie to him about her obvious lack of true family ties to the O'Connells. She was hopeful that, if such was the case, she had passed. "This is our cabin," she said, stopping outside of the door. "Thank you so much for walking with us."

"Certainly," he replied. "Hope to see you soon, Miss... what is your surname?"

As if on cue, Lizzy began to fuss. "Oh, dear. I'm so sorry. Thanks again," Meg said, bouncing the baby and disappearing into the cabin as quickly as possible. Once the door was shut, she leaned back against it, breathing a sigh of relief. Hopefully, her avoidance of the question didn't come across as rude, and Mr. Lane would only assume she was in a hurry to get the baby back to sleep. As if she had only whimpered in order to assist her aunt, Baby Lizzy fell back into a deep slumber, and even when Meg went to lay her on the bed, she did not stir. "Thank you, little angel," Meg whispered, smoothing her baby hair and kissing her gently on the top of the head before pulling the blankets around her.

However, as he made his way back up the stairs, Jonathan's suspicions continued to grow. Who was this woman that she would so blatantly avoid any question pertaining to her name? Why did she own such an expensive robe? Her hands were soft and smooth, as if she had never worked a day in her life, and the fact that she was unwilling to discuss any sort of labor, prior or future, seemed odd as well. While it didn't necessarily matter if Meg was hiding something if Charlie's only intent was to spend some time with her on the boat, he knew his friend a bit better than that. Therefore, it seemed important to know as much information about Aunty Meg as possible before Charlie became even more intrigued by her.

Ruth was certain she had seen a dawfin at last, though no one else in her party could vouch for the accuracy of her eyesight. Nevertheless, if she was happy, they were happy. Once the spotting was complete, she bounded from Charlie's arms and began to play with her mother's scarf again, throwing it up in the air and catching it as the adults leaned against the railing and chatted.

"What sort of work do you do, Daniel?" Charlie asked, leaning on one elbow.

"Carpentry, mostly," Daniel replied in his thick Irish accent. "Basically, anythin' I can do with my hands, though."

"Do you have anything lined up once you get to New York?"

"Not yet," Daniel admitted. "We had been plannin' to relocate for a while, but not so soon..."

Kelly interrupted before her husband said too much. "We jumped at the chance to book passage on the *Titanic*."

If Charlie thought Kelly's quick response was odd, he didn't let on. "I understand that," he replied. "Well, my father is always looking for able-bodied men. I'm sure we can find you something at the factory, if you're interested."

Daniel looked at Kelly, smiles spreading across both of their faces. "That would be wonderful!" Daniel exclaimed. "Thank you so much!" He stuck out his hand, which Charlie took. "I can't tell you how much it means to my family, just to know I'd have work lined up."

"Certainly," Charlie replied, dismissively. "There's family housing near the factory as well. My father believes in taking good care of his workers. Unless, of course, you already have arrangements."

"No," Kelly admitted. "I mean, I have a cousin who lives somewhere in the Bronx, and he said we could stay there for a spell if we need to, but my goodness, Mr. Ashton, to have a job for Daniel and a place to stay when we arrive... Well, God bless you, sir." Kelly wrapped her arms around him, tears beginning to stream down her face.

"It's really no trouble," Charlie assured her as she stepped back "And while Daniel will earn a decent enough wage that you can stay home with the girls, should you ever find yourself wanting to work outside of the home, I'm sure we can find you something, too. We employ lots of women as well."

"I don't even know what to say," Kelly replied wiping at tears. "Maybe Meg..." she began without thinking, but then stopped. Of course, Meg wouldn't want to work for Charlie Ashton. "Oh, but, I think... I'll speak to her."

Charlie looked at her rather oddly, unsure as to why she stopped so abruptly, but before he could question her further, he realized Ruth was gone. "Where did Ruth go?" he asked, looking around for her. She had been standing in front of them only a moment before. Now, she was nowhere to be seen.

Kelly and Daniel could not see her anywhere either. "Ruth?" Kelly yelled, her voice becoming shrill with panic. "Ruth Ann O'Connell!" she screamed at the top of her lungs.

Just then, Charlie spotted her. She was climbing on the railing a few hundred yards down the deck, just about to throw one chubby little leg over the side. Daniel was pointing and yelling, an indicator that he saw her, too, and he was slightly closer. All three took off running, pushing their way through the crowd. She was smiling, and her sweet baby voice echoed, "Horsey!" as if she were simply going to ride on the railing. However, just as she was about to put her bottom down on the handrail, she slipped. It was as if it was happening in slow motion. Charlie could see her expression change from delight to terror as she began to tumble over the side. As her father and newly-found uncle made a dive for her, the men careened into each other. Charlie heard a loud snap as Daniel hit the hard wooden boat deck, but Charlie was able to extend his left hand just enough to flip Ruth back toward the inside of the boat. With the change of direction, her momentum was slowed, and he scooped her up just in time to prevent the same sort of impact her daddy had suffered when he collided with the unforgiving promenade.

Even before he could sit her up straight, her mother was there. "Ruth Ann! Do you have any idea what almost happened? You almost fell overboard! That water is freezing! You would have died, Ruth! You would have **died**!"

Charlie put his arm around Kelly to steady her. "She's all right," he assured her, knowing that any parent would be beside him or herself in such a situation, yet Ruth was already bawling loudly, and Charlie could see no reason to further scare her. "Take a deep breath, Mummy," he said as calmly as possible.

Kelly pulled her child to her chest, tears streaming down her face. "I don't know how to thank you," she said to Charlie.

Before Charlie could reply, they realized that, though he had pulled himself to his feet, Daniel was not quite unscathed. His arm was hanging at an awkward position. "Daniel! Are you injured?" Charlie asked.

Once again, Kelly shrieked in horror. "Is it broken?" she asked, holding Ruth's head so she couldn't see.

"I'm afraid it might be," Daniel said, gritting his teeth against the obvious pain.

"Let's get you to the hospital," Charlie recommended. "Kelly, why don't you take Ruth back to your cabin? I'll make sure that Daniel is well taken care of."

"Are you certain?" she asked as Charlie was already leading her husband away.

"Quite," he assured her. "We'll have him fixed up in no time."

Kelly couldn't help but give Ruth a lecture as they made their way back to the cabin. She wasn't sure precisely how much the child could hear since she continued to wail the entire time, but it somehow made her feel slightly better. Just as she reached the stairs, she literally ran into Jonathan making his way back up to the promenade.

"Is everything all right?" he asked, clearly wondering why Ruth was so upset. "Where's Daniel?'

"Oh, Mr. Jonathan," Kelly said, pausing at the top of the stairwell. "We've had quite the adventure. This one thought it would be a fine idea to treat the railin' like a horsey, till she almost landed in the drink. And then my husband slipped in an attempt to save her and broke his arm."

"Oh, my!" Jonathan exclaimed. "How bad is it?"

"Quite terrible, I'm afraid," she replied, her lips drawn, thoughts of losing the job he had just been offered crossing her mind. "Mr. Ashton took him to the hospital to get it set, but...," she felt tears stinging her eyes again, and it was all she could do to push them back.

"I'm sure Charlie will make sure he receives excellent care," Jonathan assured her.

Kelly nodded. "I know. It's just... Mr. Ashton offered Daniel a job, but now... now...."

Jonathan rested his hand on Kelly's shoulder. "Don't worry about that," he said. "If Charlie says Daniel has a job, he has a job."

"But what sort of work can a man do with only one arm?" she asked, unable to hold back the tears any longer.

"Plenty," Jonathan smiled. "Don't worry. We'll find things that he can do with only one arm. I'm sure your husband is a hard worker. Rest assured, the Ashton's take care of their people."

Kelly temporarily let go of Ruth with one hand so that she could swipe at her eyes, a smile finally lighting up her face as the truth of Jonathan's words sank in. "Thank you," she sniffled.

"It'll be all right, I promise," Jonathan said, patting her lightly on the shoulder. "And you, missy," he said to Ruth, "best mind your mum better. That water is cold, and this boat is moving very quickly."

Ruth's cries had turned into sobs by now, and she choked out, "Yes, Mr. Jonaffin," in her soft voice before reburying her head in her mother's neck.

"What about your sister?" Jonathan asked nonchalantly. "Do you think she'd want to work for the Ashtons as well?"

"Oh, I don't know," Kelly said, attempting to be more cautious this time. "Meg's got a bit of money saved, but I don't know precisely what her plans are."

"Well, if she wants a job, I'm sure we can find her one."

"I'll be sure to let her know," Kelly replied. "Again, thank you so much."

"Are you sure you don't need any help getting Ruth back to the cabin?" he asked.

"No, I've got her," Kelly said, mustering a smile. "I may have to carry her like this for the rest of our journey to make sure she doesn't break away again, but I've got her for certain as of now."

Jonathan nodded and then continued on his way, glancing over his shoulder to make sure she cleared the stairs, which she did. *Why didn't Kelly correct me when I used the term sister? And why does Meg have money saved from a job she refuses to discuss?* he wondered as he made his way to the hospital. There were just so many unusual pieces to this puzzle. It seemed the more he learned about this O'Connell family, the more questions he had.

CHAPTER 7

"It's definitely broken," Dr. J. Edward Simpson assured Daniel once he reached the hospital located on D Deck, which was just one deck below where the incident had taken place.

Daniel had already ascertained that bit of information, but hearing the medical expert confirm it made it no less difficult to swallow. "What now?" he asked.

"Well, first I'll set it, which will likely be quite painful, then I'll cast it, which will take quite some time, and then in a month or so, depending upon how it heals, you can have a doctor in New York, or wherever you'll be residing, remove the cast," Dr. Simpson explained.

"A month?" Daniel exclaimed, looking at Charlie and shaking his head in disbelief.

"It'll be all right," Charlie assured him.

"But how am I goin' to work with a cast on my arm?" Daniel questioned, rubbing his good hand along his forehead and into his sand-colored hair.

"Don't worry about that. There are a lot of jobs you can do with one arm. Listen, right now, you need to focus on feeling better so you can make it back downstairs to your wife and daughters. Let Dr. Simpson do his job, and let me worry about everything else, all right?"

"I don't know what to say," Daniel began, a look of gratitude on his rugged face.

"This isn't charity," Charlie reminded him. "As far as I'm concerned, you're an employee now, so I need you fixed up and back on the job."

"Yes, sir," Daniel replied with a grin, despite the enormous pain. "Still, I never expected..."

"Well, as much trouble as that little girl of yours is turning out to be, you can at least be thankful that she brought us together," Charlie replied. It appeared as if Dr. Simpson was ready to get to work. Turning his attention that way, he asked, "Is there anything I can do to help, Dr. Simpson?"

"Yes, Mr. Ashton, if you don't mind, holding him still would be quite helpful," the doctor replied.

Charlie wasn't quite sure how qualified he was for such a procedure, but he didn't think it could be too difficult, so he got into position as directed by the middle-aged physician.

After a few moments of feeling the break, Dr. Simpson said, "Now, Mr. O'Connell, this is going to hurt. A lot."

As the doctor began to force the bone back into place, Charlie felt Daniel's entire upper body stiffen and found it almost impossible to hold him still. However, just when Charlie was quite certain Daniel could take no more, the doctor was done. "There we go," he was saying calmly, as if he had not just made a grown man cry. "Now, I will start to work on the cast. It will likely take at least six hours to dry."

"Six hours!" Daniel repeated, wide eyes, still brushing tears from his cheeks.

"Possibly longer in this humid air," Dr. Simpson admitted in his even tone.

"I can't sit here for six hours," Daniel implored, shaking his head.

"I'm afraid you'll have to," Dr. Simpson stated as he readied himself for the casting. "I can't risk letting you get up before it dries. If you displace the bone, we'll have to set it again. And I'm fairly certain you do not want me to have to do that."

"No, sir," Daniel answered quickly.

"Good, then let's begin," the doctor replied and set about casting the broken arm.

"I'll go speak to Kelly and make sure she knows you're all right. Then, I'll come back and check on you," Charlie offered.

"Again, thank you so much, Mr. Ashton," Daniel said, careful not to move his arm one iota as Dr. Simpson worked.

"Certainly," Charlie said before disappearing out the door.

Charlie met Jonathan just a few steps out of the hospital ward, headed his direction, a worried expression on his face. "Jonathan, did you get Meg and the baby back to their quarters safely?" he asked.

"Yes, they're fine," he assured his friend. "I ran into Kelly. Is Daniel doing all right?"

"He is, though it was a pretty terrible break," he confirmed. "It's been a long time since I've seen a tough man like Daniel O'Connell cry, but setting that bone seemed awfully painful."

"That's too bad," Jonathan replied, nodding his head politely at a couple as they passed by in the crowded corridor. "I'm glad it wasn't something more serious. And that you caught Ruth before she fell overboard."

Charlie shook his head. "That girl is something else." Burying his hands in his pockets, he let out a deep sigh and added, "I hope she learned her lesson this time."

"She's certainly a little spitfire," Jonathan agreed, scratching his head.

"I'm going to go let Kelly know how Daniel is doing and that the doctor said it will take about six hours for the cast to set," Charlie continued.

"Six hours?" the valet repeated. "That sounds awful. What can I do?"

"Nothing right now, I guess," Charlie admitted. "We should probably go check on him in a few hours, though. Do you know the O'Connell's room number?"

"Yes," Jonathan replied. "It's E 204." Charlie repeated the number, and then Jonathan added, "All right, I'll head back to my room for a while then. See you in a bit."

Charlie nodded and headed off toward the stairs that led to E Deck thinking, if nothing else, at least he'd have another opportunity to see Meg.

❧

"JESUS, MARY, AND JOSEPH," Kelly exclaimed just above a whisper as she made her way into the cabin. "You'll never believe what your niece has done now." She plopped Ruth onto her bed, handing her a doll that had been Meg's at one time. "Lie down girly, and say your prayers, thankin' the Lord that He kept you safe."

Meg had been lying on her bed reading a book, but she had all of her attention focused on Kelly now. "What happened?" she asked.

Kelly checked on Lizzy, who was still sleeping, and then sat down on the edge of Meg's bed, careful not to hit her head. "She almost fell overboard pretendin' the railin' was a horsey," Kelly explained. Even retelling it now seemed painful, and Meg's eyes widened in horror at each word. "Just as she was about to tumble into the water, Charlie reached her and pulled her back over. If he hadn't been there, well, I think she'd be gone."

"Oh, my!" Meg exclaimed, her eyes wide in astonishment. "How did she.... What .... Did she...."

"She slipped away again. We took our eyes off of her for just a moment, and when we turned back, she was gone. Then we spotted her climbin'. I tell you, Meg, I don't know what to do. And Daniel slipped and broke his arm. He's at the hospital now gettin' it fixed up."

"What? Is he all right?" Once again, Meg could hardly believe her ears.

"I hope so. I don't know. I needed to get her back here. Charlie took him. I just...." She paused and turned to face her friend before continuing. "Meg, it's as if God placed him directly into our lives, you know?"

Meg wasn't sure what to make of that comment, so she dismissed it. "I'm glad nothing worse happened," she finally said, still shaking her head.

"And he offered Daniel a job at his father's company. I was certain he'd lose that job for sure. But I ran into Jonathan on the way back here, and Jonathan said not to worry about it. They'll find him some-thin' he can do with just the one arm for now. Here we were, hopin' and prayin' God would lead us in right direction, and the same man we're runnin' away from is the one to offer us a solution. What are the chances of that?"

"I have money," Meg reminded her. "We have enough to last a while, until we find work."

"Oh, I know, Meggy, but we didn't want to take your money. And Charlie has offered us a place to live nearby the factory. You, too, of course. He even said you could work there if you wanted to, though I didn't think you would," Kelly explained.

Meg grew a bit alarmed. "What did you tell him?"

"Nothin'. Only that I didn't know—that we'd have to ask you," Kelly replied. "Why?"

Meg realized she'd grown a bit snippy, and she didn't mean to. "No reason," she replied, trying to keep her voice calmer. "It's just, Jonathan was asking about me working as well, and I want to make sure we are consistent, that's all. I don't want him growing suspicious. I told him we aren't really sisters."

"You did?" Kelly inquired, her freckled brow creasing.

"Yes. He asked, and well, it seems pretty obvious just by looking at us that we aren't really related. We don't even have the same accent," Meg reminded her.

"True," Kelly said. Hesitating at first, she finally continued, "Well, he referred to you as my sister a bit ago, and I didn't correct him. I'm sure he'll just assume that I obviously think of you as a sister. It's nothin' I'm sure."

Meg wasn't quite as positive, but she was glad to have that information. "You're probably right," she agreed. "But if he says anything else, be sure to let him know we aren't attempting to cover anything up— not that anyway."

"All right," Kelly agreed. "But Meg, if Daniel is to be workin' for Mr. Ashton, you do realize it will be quite difficult for us to keep up this charade indefinitely."

"I know," Meg agreed. "But we'll figure it out. It'll be easier if I can find my own place and employer sooner rather than later. If we're not together, there'd be no reason for him to keep asking questions, and you can just forget about your old life in Southampton."

"What? And forget about you. That's rubbish, love. You know I wouldn't have even come to America if it weren't for you," Kelly reminded her.

"No, not forget me. Of course, not," Meg assured her, though on the inside she wasn't certain of her words. "Just separate us, that's all. We'll sort it all out. I am thankful that Charlie offered Daniel a job, however. And I want to do everything I can to make sure I don't mess this up for the pair of you."

Kelly nodded. The thought had certainly crossed her mind. If Charlie were to discover Meg's true identity, he could become so angry that he no longer wanted to employ Daniel, which would put them right back in the tough spot they'd been in before. No, it was best if Meg kept her secret. And if that meant avoiding Charlie, then, perhaps, Meg was right about that after all. "Well, I'm exhausted from all this," Kelly said, patting her friend on the arm. "I'm gonna hoist myself atop Daniel's bunk there and take a wee nap."

"All right then. Sweet dreams," Meg replied. The idea of taking a nap seemed a bit appealing to her as well, except for sleeping always brought the threat of the nightmares, even during the day time, so she turned her attention back to her book. Soon, the sound of Kelly's soft snoring filled the small space, and she couldn't help but chuckle at how familiar the sleeping patterns were of all three of the O'Connell women.

A soft rapping at the door a bit later brought her back from the book. She was expecting either Daniel's return or an update at some point, and since Daniel would not knock on his own door, she was praying it was Jonathan. Of course, upon opening the door, she quickly ascertained that it was not. "Charlie," she said quietly. He was smiling at her but didn't speak, and she realized he had considered the fact that the baby was sleeping. She glanced back over her shoulder, hoping perhaps Kelly had awoken and could rescue her. All three of her room-mates were still sawing logs. She stepped out into the hallway, carefully closing the door behind her. "How is Daniel?"

He stepped to the side a bit, as if attempting to put more distance between himself and the sleeping baby before answering. "He's in a lot of pain, but Dr. Simpson was able to set the break. He said it will take quite some time for the cast to dry, possibly up to six hours."

"Six hours?" Meg repeated in a harsh whisper. "My goodness. What's he going to do for six hours? Can he come back here?"

"No, the doctor said he couldn't move until it's dry. Hopefully it won't take longer in the humid air," he replied.

So far Meg had avoided looking directly into his eyes, but she caught them just then, and the response she was about to give was lost somewhere between her mind and her mouth. She caught her breath, looked away somehow, and began to reformulate a coherent sentence.

"Are you all right?" he asked, innocently placing his hand on her arm.

Meg's eyes immediately went from his hand to his eyes and then back again. Rather than remove his hand, he gave her arm a gentle squeeze, and she realized he wasn't deterred at all by her hesitation. Eventually, she said, "I'm fine, thank you; it's just ...a lot to take in."

"I know," he agreed. "I guess Kelly told you about Ruth?"

She nodded, aware that his hand was still on her arm, though her eyes were now transfixed on a dirty spot on the floor. Her words caught in the back of her throat, her emotions overwhelming her. Thoughts of Ruth plunging overboard, of the pain Daniel must be in, of this man she was supposed to marry standing before her, his hand innocently resting on her arm, having no idea she was a liar... a cheater... a coward.

"Meg?"

She looked up at him again, another mistake. His eyes showed nothing but concern. As she continued to stare, speechless, his free hand came up and gently pushed a lock of hair behind her ear, his fingertips softly brushing her cheek as he did so.

"It will be all right, I promise."

She nodded as he withdrew his hand from her hair. And unlike Mary Margaret Westmoreland, Charles J. Ashton kept his promises. "I should go..." she finally managed to choke out.

"Okay," he said softly, a bit of confusion evident on his handsome face.

"Kelly, um, will want to know," she continued.

He nodded, his hand sliding down her arm, taking her hand, interlacing her thin fingers in his. Despite the desperate need to pull away, she continued to stand there, wondering if, with one step forward, perhaps, he might lean down and kiss her. As much as she wanted to take that step, she knew regardless of his motivation, whether he was genuinely attracted to her or simply sowing some wild oats, she had already visited enough misery upon this kind and considerate gentleman. What Charlie didn't realize was it was in his best interest to forget he'd ever known Mary Margaret, that he'd ever met Meg. It took everything she had not to press on, but, eventually, she was able to slip her hand out of his, and fumbling for the door behind her, she managed to say, "Thank you, Charlie," before she ducked back inside.

Charlie stood in the hallway outside of her door for a long moment, contemplating what had just happened. For some reason, Meg was hesitant to let him know how she felt, but he was quite certain that she was just as attracted to him as he was to her. Perhaps she was leery of getting involved with someone of a higher social class. Perhaps she was on her way to meet some beau in America. He wasn't quite sure, but he was determined to find out what her reservations were and overcome them. While Jonathan and others might be encouraging him to have a bit of a tryst whilst on the boat, a girl like Meg warranted more devotion than that, and he was no longer in a situation where he cared what the other socialites thought of him and his relationships.

CHAPTER 8

Daniel had returned from the hospital just before dinner time still in a lot of pain, but his arm was wrapped up tight in a cast, and Dr. Simpson assured him that it would heal just fine so long as he kept the cast dry and went to a doctor within a few weeks of disembarking. Charlie and Jonathan had both stopped by to see him in the hospital as he waited for the cast to dry, and Meg had watched the girls for a bit so that Kelly could as well.

When Ruth saw her daddy's cast she cried, saying she was, "So, so, so, so sorry, Daddy," and Kelly took it as another opportunity to drive home the idea that she must stay with Mummy, Daddy, or Aunty Meg at all times to which she had added, "Or Uncle Charlie. Or Mr. Jonaffin." Her mother gave in but insisted that the list could not be lengthened to add anyone else, and Ruth agreed that she would never run off again.

Daniel was too tired to accompany them to dinner, so the ladies took the girls and went to the Third Class Dining Hall on their own. Once again, Ruth was having a hard time eating her food, insisting that everything was yucky. Meg couldn't help but think about how different things were in First Class where everyone had to be so prim and proper. Any sort of misbehavior would be cause for severe punishment.

She had met the wide end of a wooden spoon many times over similar incidents at Ruth's age. But Kelly and Daniel chose to parent with a more loving approach, and Meg could appreciate that. She hoped that, if she were ever given the opportunity to have her own children, she would find a way to be firm but loving.

"I heard there's to be a dance in the Third Class lounge this evening," Kelly said, smiling and raising her eyebrows at Meg suggestively as she balanced Lizzy on her lap and attempted to eat at the same time.

Meg looked at her with a questioning expression. She began to move her food around her plate with her fork, similar to the way her niece was protesting the presence of broccoli on her plate just now. "And?" she asked once she realized Kelly wasn't going to say more on her own.

"And I think you should go," she replied. "It might be fun. You could find a good lookin' fellow to twirl around the dance floor with."

Meg scoffed. "Me? Attend a Third Class dance? I don't think so."

"I like to dance," Ruth chimed in.

"Hush, little one," Kelly shot back. "You're not goin' anywhere after the stunt you pulled today."

Ruth's face fell, and she leaned back in her chair, arms crossed. "I never get to have any fun."

Kelly ignored her and returned her attention to Meg. "What's the matter? Third Class gentlemen not good enough for you, then?"

She knew Kelly was joking, but the irony of the statement was not lost on her. It had, after all, been a Third Class gentleman who had essentially gotten her into this predicament in the first place. "You know that's not what I meant," she replied. "Let me rephrase that. Me? Attend a dance? I don't think so."

"Why not? You were always the belle of the ball back home. Always got your dance card full. Listen, darlin' I know you don't want to think about this just yet, but you've got to consider findin' yourself a good fellow sooner rather than later."

She was right; Meg didn't want to think about it. "Not yet," she said, shaking her head. "Too soon."

"What about Uncle Charlie?" Ruth asked, suddenly out of her solemn state again.

Meg looked at Kelly questioningly. The girl's mother shrugged, indicating she'd said nothing, and then Meg returned her attention to the tot. "What's that darling?" she asked.

"You can't go to the ball and dance with some other fellow. You have to marry Uncle Charlie," she explained matter-of-factly.

Meg held back a laugh. "Ruthy, darling, why would you say such a thing?"

"Because he loves you," she shrugged. "And you love him."

Once again, Kelly indicated she had no idea where this was coming from.

"Ruth, Mr. Charlie is a nice man, but I don't think Aunty Meg is going to marry him, sweetheart," Meg assured her, patting her little hand.

With an air of nonchalance, Ruth shrugged. "You'll see," she said, as if she knew her statements to be fact.

"Well, there's no way I'm going to the dance by myself anyway," Meg declared, finally taking a bite of her chicken.

"Fine," Kelly shrugged. "I'll go with you."

࿐

"ONE DOESN'T SIMPLY BOW out of an obligation to meet J. J. Astor in the Smoking Lounge after dinner, Jonathan, you know that," Charlie was explaining as he finished dressing for the evening meal.

"Why not? Who is more important right now, Mr. Astor or Miss Meg?" the valet asked, slipping Charlie's jacket on and brushing off any stray lint.

"That's not the point," Charlie insisted, adjusting his cufflinks. "Chances are Meg won't even attend this party. She seems to rather keep to herself."

"All I'm saying is that it's supposed to be quite the event, and chances are she will be there, and it might give you the opportunity to talk to her in private, should you wish to do so. And if you get there and she is not present, go to her room, and invite her!"

"Oh, is that all your saying, then?" Charlie remarked, straightening his tie in the mirror. Turning away from his own reflection, he met Jonathan's gaze. "Look," he said, "I am definitely intrigued by Meg, that's for certain. But she acted so peculiarly in the hallway this afternoon. It was as if she wanted me to kiss her—but then she ran away before I could even try."

"Maybe she just doesn't want to come off as too easy," Jonathan offered.

"I don't think that's it," Charlie replied, turning back to the mirror one last time and running his hand across his shoulder. "Not that she's trying to come across as easy.... You know what I mean. I think there's something else, some bit of information I'm not privy to."

"I would agree with that," Jonathan acknowledged. "There are bits and pieces that seem rather odd to me, as well."

"Such as?"

"Well, her last name for example. We don't know what it is, and whenever we make inquiry, she changes the subject. We know she has money, but she won't talk about work. She admits she's not Kelly's sister, but Kelly says she is. It's all rather odd, isn't it?"

"Maybe. Maybe not. I don't know," Charlie admitted, crossing his arms. "I mean, she may be wondering why someone of my social class is even pursuing her. She probably thinks I'm only after a short roll in the hay. Couldn't blame her for thinking so. Most men in my situation would only be interested in that."

"And what are you interested in exactly?" Jonathan questioned.

Charlie considered his own previous statement and the question before answering. "Well, more than that, then, I suppose."

"So, tell me again why you're planning on spending your time with J. J. Astor instead of Meg then?"

Charlie smoothed back his hair. "You have a point. All right, I'll pay a token visit to the Smoking Lounge and then come back here to change into something less formal. We'll go see if this party is all it's cracked up to be. But if Meg's not there, I'm not going to show up at her door, risk waking the baby, just to beg her to attend a party I'm not invited to. Deal?"

"Deal," Jonathan agreed.

Dinner was just as much a whispering, staring match as breakfast had been, but by now, Charlie no longer cared at all what the other First Class passengers had to say, and a few times when he caught gloved hands covering faces, obviously speaking about him, he waved across the room, causing the mumbling ninnies to blush in embarrassment.

"Heard you had a bit of excitement on the Third Class promenade this morning, Charlie," Molly mentioned with a knowing smile halfway through the event.

"We did," Charlie affirmed. "Lots of excitement indeed, Ms. Molly."

"What happened?" one of the older gentlemen at the table asked.

Charlie realized all eyes were suddenly on him. They were probably wondering what he was doing on the Third Class promenade in the first place. Well, if they wanted to know, they had better muster the courage to ask. Otherwise, he would answer the question with as little detail as possible. "A child almost fell off the railing, and when her father and I went to retrieve her, we collided and he broke his arm."

"Oh, my," the gentlemen's wife exclaimed. "Was the child all right?"

"She was fine, as was her father, after a nice long visit to the hospital," he assured them.

"You know, these Steerage passengers just don't have a handle on their children," a shrewd looking woman at the far end of the table offered to those sitting closest to her. "You'd never see that sort of behavior out of a First Class passenger's child." There were several nods of agreement.

Charlie couldn't help but take offense. After all, this woman was talking about his Ruth. "I don't think it's fair to make such generalizations," he said calmly.

"Oh, please," she continued, "all one has to do is peer below deck, and you'll see those children running around like wild animals. Our children, on the other hand know how to play properly."

"Mrs. Appleton, is it?" Charlie asked, waiting for her to nod an acknowledgement before continuing. "Saying that all Third Class children are wild animals while all First Class children are well behaved is rather like saying all Third Class women are respectful and courteous while all First Class women are gossip mongers who can't keep their long noses out of other people's business. Just because I can name several dozen examples of the latter doesn't make my generalization truth, does it?"

The woman looked very offended. "Are you saying that members of your own class don't know how to keep to themselves better than the fodder on the decks below us, Mr. Ashton?" she asked.

"No, of course not, Mrs. Appleton," he replied. "That's my point exactly. Such statements only make one sound foolish, wouldn't you agree? Therefore, I shall be sure not to lump you and yours into any preconceived groups if you think you can do the same. What do you say, Mrs. Appleton? Seems like a fair bargain, doesn't it?"

"Of course, I can," she agreed. "But I will say, you seem a bit bitter in regards to woman of stature all of a sudden, Mr. Ashton," she said haughtily, a knowing smile playing at her lips.

"And the fact that you would say it proves my summation without me having to make any sort of statement at all," he replied.

Molly burst out laughing, clapping loudly as well, which drew the attention of many of the surrounding tables. "That was a good one, Charlie!" she exclaimed. "I really like you, young man," she continued.

Charlie could feel the color rising in his cheeks, not from the exchange with Mrs. Appleton, who was of little consequence to him socially or professionally, but because of the attention Molly's boisterousness always seemed to draw. "Thank you, Mrs. Brown," he said quietly.

"From all the accounts I heard, and there were a lot of them—after all, I am a First Class female passenger—you were a hero today. You saved that little girl's life, and you helped her daddy to the hospital. Now, that's the kind of young men our society needs to raise, regardless of stature or social class."

Someone at the other end of the table proposed a toast, which even Mrs. Appleton was inclined to participate in, and Charlie did his best not to show how extremely uncomfortable he was. Luckily, as soon as the toast was over, someone changed the subject, and he was able to sink back into oblivion without anyone noticing.

When dinner was over, he was obliged to walk Mrs. Brown to the staircase before making his way to the Smoking Lounge. Mr. Astor had caught him earlier and reminded him of his commitment, as if he could have forgotten. "Don't you worry about ol' Mrs. Appleton," Molly assured him. "A lot of nerve she's got talkin' about kids. She don't even have any."

"I shouldn't have gotten so offended," Charlie admitted. "It's just, she doesn't know the parents, and she doesn't know the child."

"And you do?" Molly asked. Charlie nodded. "Good. Took my advice then, did you?"

"Not exactly," he replied. "Something like that."

Molly was grinning from ear to ear. "That's my boy!" she said. "Ooh, when do I get to meet her?"

"I didn't even say there was a her, Molly," he replied, trying to back his way out of her game of Twenty Questions.

"Course you did," she replied. "Invite her to dinner tomorrow night."

"There's no way she'll come," he replied sharply.

"Course she will. Who could resist you and your boyish charm?"

He was afraid she might reach up and pinch his cheek at any moment. "She wouldn't have anything suitable to wear," he reminded her.

"That's all right. I'll find her a nice dress. Nothin' I have'll probably fit her, but I got friends. Can you imagine the looks on the faces of those busybodies when you walk in here with some beautiful girl they don't even know? That'll set their heads a spinnin'. Come on now, Charlie. Let's not miss this opportunity to mess with their minds."

Charlie looked down at her, a questioning expression on his face. "I thought you wanted to invite her for her own sake, not the opportunity to screw around with other people's sense of entitlement."

"Oh, that, too," she replied. "Don't make me follow you around all day tomorrow until we bump into her now, you hear?"

"I'll see what I can do," he promised as they reached the grand staircase.

"That's my boy!" she said again, giving him a quick kiss on the cheek before heading upstairs, leaving him shaking his head, wondering what he'd gotten himself—and Meg—into. He was quite certain there was nothing he could say to convince her to join him, but he would try, not only for her own sake (after all, how many opportunities did a Steerage passenger have to attend dinner in the First Class Banquet Hall?) but he had to admit he would also like to see the confused expressions of the gossip mongers' faces as he escorted a beautiful—unknown—woman to dinner.

It had been easier than he expected to find his way out of the Smoking Lounge. In fact, J.J. left before he did, explaining to everyone that Madeline was not feeling well and that he needed to return to their chambers to attend to his wife. He was able to slip out just before 10:00, and despite his timing, Jonathan was waiting for him upon his arrival back at his room, his clothing laid out, ready to go.

Once he was dressed more appropriately, though still in a dress shirt and slacks, he looked at himself one more time in the mirror. "You sure about this?" he asked Jonathan, who was dressed in a similar outfit.

"Absolutely," he replied. "Let's go to a real party."

CHAPTER 9

Kelly refused any of the several beers gentlemen began offering her the moment she and Meg walked in the door. She was still nursing Lizzy, after all, and she'd noticed the baby was a bit groggy if she drank anything at all even a few hours before she fed her. Meg, on the other hand, had accepted the first drink she'd been offered, which had cost her an obligatory dance with a rather large Scottish lad named Titus, but the glasses were tall, and she was able to make that drink last long enough she was not forced to accept any of the other offers that came her way.

Occasionally, Kelly consented to cut a rug with the more attractive men that asked, but for the most part, she simply flashed her wedding band in the direction of those who'd have her hand, and they'd move along. Meg didn't mind telling the men no directly. In fact, she wished she'd done more of it in her former life.

"We really shouldn't stay too long," Meg yelled over the clang of the drums and the din of the hand organ. "You'll be regretting staying out so late when your little ones want you up at the crack of dawn."

"Don't be such a stick in the mud," Kelly replied. "This is supposed to be fun. There's a handsome fellow over there. Why don't you see if you can catch his eye? Maybe he'll ask you to dance."

"He's missing most of his bottom teeth," Meg pointed out, a look of disgust on her face.

"Ugh, you're sooo picky," Kelly replied. "Maybe he's a prize fighter."

"Maybe he doesn't own a toothbrush," she retaliated. They were huddled in a corner toward the back of the room, perhaps because neither of them really wanted to dance anyway, but Meg liked to watch other people, and she was having fun observing some very flirtatious girls interact with what could only be called the most handsome group of men in relation to those around them.

"I think there are some Second Class passengers here," Kelly noted. "Maybe even a few First."

"Do you think they're just here to laugh at us?" Meg asked.

"No, they're here because they know Third Class passengers know how to have a grand time. Not us, of course. Certainly not you."

"Hey, I know how to kick up my heels and enjoy myself," Meg shot back.

"No, you know how to attend a ball. You don't know how to loosen up and dance," Kelly replied.

"I danced. I could dance. I don't want to dance," Meg explained, crossing her arms across the borrowed navy-blue and white checked dress she was wearing. She had only drank about half of her beer, but she was wondering if it was beginning to affect her thinking because she was aware that her speech didn't quite sound as sophisticated as it normally did.

"Well, you might want to dance now," Kelly muttered, peering out across the crowd.

"What's that?" Meg asked, attempting to see what, or who, she was looking at. Clearly, he saw her at the same time that she saw him, and there was no avoiding eye contact or attempting to sneak away. After an audible catch in her breath, Meg finally managed to mutter, "Why is Charlie here?"

"I don't know," Kelly replied. "But he is. What are you goin' to do?"

"What can I do?" Meg replied, pulling her eyes off of him at last and shrugging her shoulders. "He's coming over. I can't hide. Should I grab some random fellow and ask him to dance?"

"Yeah, that wouldn't seem strange at all," Kelly said, shaking her head. "Too late now."

"Well, fancy meeting you here," Charlie said as he stepped directly in front of her. While his attire was less formal than usual, he certainly stood out amongst the crowd, and Meg lost the ability to speak momentarily as she stared at him in awe and confusion. Jonathan was there as well, standing behind Charlie, an odd smile on his face as he chuckled quietly to himself.

Kelly was not, however, at a loss for words. "It's our party," she reminded him with a mischievous wink.

"That's true," Charlie admitted, drawing his hands out of his trouser pockets and crossing his arms across his chest as if in contemplation. "But I wasn't sure if you would be here, what with the small children, injured husband, and all."

"Well, I couldn't let Meg come by herself," Kelly explained feigning offense.

Charlie nodded, a small smile playing at the corners of his mouth. He took a step closer to Meg, and leaning in so she could hear him above the music, he asked, "Do you like to dance then, Meg?"

His proximity caught her a bit off guard, so before answering, Meg took another swig of her beer, hoping to gain some liquid courage. She wiped the foam off her mouth on the back of her hand, before taking a deep breath and replying simply, "Not with them." She shifted her gaze away from Charlie, past Jonathan, across the room at Titus who was dancing with a small dark-haired woman, his heavily-browed eyes darting Meg's direction on occasion, as if to let her know he was still claiming her as his girl.

Charlie glanced over his shoulder momentarily, considering Meg's other prospects before returning his attention to her and mumbling, "Okay, then." By the variety of potential suitors in the crowd, those clearly members of Steerage and some dressed well enough to be Second or even First Class passengers, he was not able to tell whether she was referring to a specific group of men, or just men in general. After a moment of contemplation, he finally asked, "If you don't want to dance with any of 'them,' why are you here?"

Without thinking, Meg replied, "She made me come," gesturing in

Kelly's general direction and sloshing some of her drink as she did so. She knew the beer was definitely affecting her now, but even with that information, she wasn't able to stop the flow of gibberish spewing from her lips, so she continued. "She was hoping I'd meet a nice fellow."

"Meg," Kelly warned, tugging gently on her shoulder, "I think you've had enough beer for a while, darlin'."

Meg looked at the glass in her hand, which was about two-thirds gone, and nodded, stepping over to sit it down on a nearby table.

As she turned to dispose of her beverage, Charlie stepped closer to Kelly and asked quietly, "How many has she had?"

"That's her first," Kelly admitted, "but she doesn't drink much."

"I see," Charlie replied, nodding and returning his attention to Meg who was staggering just a hair as she crossed back over to him.

"Well, if she doesn't drink, and she doesn't dance, perhaps this isn't the best way for her to spend her evening," Jonathan chimed in, speaking about her as if she wasn't there, even though she could clearly hear him above the music.

A scowl formed on Meg's pretty face. "But this is where the men are," she reminded him, placing a slightly wobbly hand on Jonathan's upper arm. "If I'm gonna meet one, like Kelly wants, I've gotta come here."

"Meggy, darlin' I don't think you quite.... She's not.... Maybe we should just be gettin' her some water," Kelly stammered, her face beginning to redden with embarrassment for her friend.

"I'll get it," Jonathan offered, gently taking Meg's small hand in his and removing it from his arm, placing it carefully on Charlie's arm instead before he disappeared into the crowd in search of something more benign for Meg to drink.

Meg's head was beginning to feel a little fuzzy, but she wasn't willing to accept the fact that one beer could cause her to act so out of character. "I'm really not that drunk," she insisted, realizing that her hand was now resting on Charlie's bicep, which was quite firm. She ran her hand along his sleeve for a second before realizing what she was doing. Drawing her hand away and looking at it in confusion, as if it had betrayed her, she quickly thrust both hands behind her back, hoping she could behave herself that way.

With a peculiar expression on his face, Charlie took a step closer to her, saying, "You seem a little tipsy." He carefully placed a hand on her arm to steady her.

"Do I?" she asked, placing her hands on his chest. "Because I don't really think I am." She glanced down at her own hands, realizing their duplicity but powerless to remove them.

Charlie was looking at her hands quizzically as well. After a moment, he replied, "I think it's fair to say you might be a little drunk, Meg."

Sighing loudly enough to be heard above the din of the percussion, Kelly looped her arm through Meg's elbow and pulled her back, saying to Charlie, "Excuse us, just a moment," before she stepped between them and said, "Meg, darlin', what are you doin'?"

"Nothing. I'm not doing anything," Meg assured her, glancing over Kelly's shoulder at Charlie, who was now standing several feet away, scratching his head in confusion and perhaps a bit of amusement.

Through clenched teeth, Kelly said very quietly, right next to her ear, "You do remember who this is, who he thinks you are, and who he doesn't suspect you are at all, right sweetie?"

Returning her attention to her friend, Meg assured her, "Yes! It's fine. I know. I'm Aunty Meg—not that other girl. I won't ruin this for you, I promise."

"You promise?" Kelly repeated, pointing at her sharply.

"Yes, I promise!" Meg assured her. Just then, she saw Jonathan was back with a glass of water. With another knowing glance and a quick nod of her head, she stepped around Kelly to meet him. "Thank you, Jonathan," she said, taking the water from him and swallowing a big gulp. "You really are so kindhearted, aren't you?"

"I guess so," he said a questioning lilt to his voice, his brow creased in confusion.

She handed the glass back to Jonathan, who looked at it oddly before sitting it on the table next to her beer. Meg's attention was no longer on the valet, however, and quickly closing the small space between them, she said, "So, Charlie, are we going to dance?" as she delicately placed her hand back on his arm.

"Well," Charlie said surveying the dance floor, "I'm not sure I know any of these steps...."

"Me neither," Meg said. A swift kick in the back of her leg from Kelly later, and she added, "I mean, not this particular style. This is more... German influenced, I think."

"Possibly," he said, trying not to laugh at her obvious improvisation. "But I thought you said you don't dance."

She was not so drunk as to miss his teasing expression. "I said I don't want to dance with them." She gestured at Titus and his friends across the room with her forehead, a playful lilt in her voice.

Charlie glanced back across the room at the group. He was certain now that he had caught their attention, and he wasn't sure if their sharp glances were due to his social status or the fact that he was clearly imposing on territory at least one of them had already claimed for his own. Nevertheless, it wasn't like Charlie to back down from a challenge. He considered leading her out to the floor, but Meg began to sway again, and he was unsure as to whether or not she was in any condition to attempt a dance. "I don't know, Meg..." he began, glancing at Kelly for an indication as to the likelihood Meg could handle a turn on the dance floor presently or not.

"All right, Mr. New Yorker," Meg said, moving her head in order to regain his attention and staring straight into his eyes, "if you don't dance, and I don't see a beer in your hand, why are *you* here?"

Charlie couldn't help but laugh. It was wonderful to see her personality shining through at last. Perhaps a bit of alcohol had done her well. Still grinning at her, he leaned in, a bit surprised when she did not retreat, and pushing her blonde locks out of the way he whispered into her ear, "To see you."

As he pulled away, she cocked her head to one side, the soft skin of her alabaster cheek brushing his and said in a breathy whisper, "Well then, dance with me."

Smiling a crooked grin, Charlie nodded, saying "All right, then, Miss Meg." Taking her hand in his, he led her out to the makeshift dance floor, muttering quietly under his breath "but you'll be sorry you asked."

Except she wasn't sorry. As the rhythm of drums and violin

increased, he wrapped one arm tightly around her waist, still holding her other hand in his and began to move her swiftly around the dance floor. Neither of them had any clue how to do the steps the Third Class passengers around them knew so well, but that didn't stop them from trying, and when they couldn't figure it out at all, Charlie would take the lead in one of the many ballroom dances he did know, which oddly enough, from his perspective, she seemed to know as well. He twirled her around with the grace of a trained, yet unchoreographed, dancer until they were both laughing so hard their sides were aching. Finally, the music shifted, the beat slowing a bit, and Charlie pulled Meg's body close to his, beads of sweat beginning to glisten on his fore-head, as he led her into a sensuous Tango.

Meg smiled a mischievous grin, and as she followed him with the expertise only one well-versed in such an intricate dance could surmise, she couldn't help but giggle at the confused expression on his hand-some face.

Charlie spun her around so that her back was pressed against him, her head resting on his shoulder. Leaning in closely, his lips pressed closely to her ear, he whispered, "How do you know the Tango?"

With a wicked smile, Meg pulled away, unfurling herself in a passionate crescendo, one arm raised above her head, the other hand still firmly grasping his. As he pulled her back toward him, she replied, "My mother taught me." Her eyes were locked on his, and rather than continuing with the intricate steps, she let him lead her in a steady rocking motion back in forth with the beat of the music. After a moment, she continued, not sure why she felt compelled to further her explanation but feeling a bit of solace in those now familiar green eyes. "Mother always loved to dance. She probably knew all of the proper steps we're supposed to be doing as well," she added as a redirection.

Charlie smiled, releasing her hand and sliding his arms around her more tightly. Still entranced by her eyes, he laughed, "You're a remark-able dancer, especially for someone who claims to have no idea what she's doing."

Meg was very aware of just how tightly he was holding her, and while she knew she should be cautious, particularly because of the alcohol she had consumed, there was something so familiar about

Charlie, so reassuring, she was neither hesitant nor apprehensive at his touch. Placing her arms around his neck she replied quietly, "Thank you. You are also highly skilled at the art of pretend dancing."

Charlie said nothing in reply, only continued to stare into her eyes, shaking his head in disbelief. As Meg leaned her head against his shoulder, her soft breathing caressing his neck, all thoughts of his life before *Titanic* began to fade, and all he could think about was how very lucky he was to have met such a remarkable young lady in such perfect timing.

Meg wasn't sure how much time had passed as she melted into the solace of Charlie's embrace, but after what could have been minutes or hours later, a sharp poking on her shoulder brought her out of her trance, and she turned to see familiar Irish eyes squinting at her. "Excuse me, for a moment, won't you Charlie?" Kelly asked as she pried Meg out of his arms, pulling her away a few steps. In a harsh whisper, she asked "Meg, darlin', what are you doin'?"

"I don't know," she replied honestly. She was fully aware that just a short time ago, she had insisted that Kelly prevent her from going anywhere near Charlie Ashton, and now, here she was wrapped in his arms, dancing the night away. "But I'm not drunk anymore, that's for certain. And... I really want to be with him." She nervously raised her hand to her mouth, beginning to chew on her fingernails as she waited for a reply, much like a young child waiting to see what punishment her mother had in store.

Kelly absently brushed Meg's hand away from her mouth, the fire in her voice evident as she asked, "So you are choosin' to break this kind man's heart? Again?"

"No, I'm not... I'll... figure it out...." Meg replied, adamantly shaking her head, her hands neatly folded in front of her.

With a loud sigh, Kelly placed both hands on Meg's shoulder and looked her squarely in the eyes. "All right, well as you do so, please bear in mind he is now my husband's employer, okay, love?"

"I know, Kell. I know," Meg assured her.

"I need to get back to the girls, so Jonathan has offered to walk me to the cabin. Do you feel all right about me leavin' you with Charlie?" Kelly asked, crossing her arms across her chest and glancing over her shoulder to where Charlie was standing, speaking to Jonathan who was now at his side.

"Yes, of course," Meg nodded.

"All right. Jonathan will probably come back once he's got me home anyhow. Please be careful, love. I don't want to see either one of you be put through any more foolishness if it can be avoided," Kelly warned

Once again, Meg nodded and gave Kelly a quick hug before she met up with Jonathan, who concluded his conversation with Charlie and gave Meg a small wave goodbye. With one last glance in Meg's general direction, Kelly made her way over to the stairwell alongside the valet and disappeared into the crowd, leaving an indecisive Meg to her own devices.

"Everything okay?" Charlie asked as he stepped over to where Meg was still standing, her eyes cast down to the floor in contemplation.

After a moment, Meg nodded. She finally pulled her eyes away from the floor, and as she leaned in, she whispered into Charlie's ear, "Can we go somewhere quieter, where we can talk? The promenade perhaps?"

"Of course," Charlie replied, raising his eyebrows in surprise. Taking her by the hand, he carefully led her over to the stairs, ignoring the jealous eyes that followed them as he did so.

Meg knew the change in location meant Jonathan wouldn't find them directly, but her conversation with Kelly had sobered her up a bit, and she concluded she had some important things to say to Charlie, things she could hardly say while gallivanting around the dance floor.

Once they reached the deck, Meg began to shiver. At first, she thought it might be because of the conversation she was about to embark upon, but then she realized just how chilly it truly was. The breeze was blowing in off of the water, and she began to wish she had brought her shawl. Charlie must have noticed just how uncomfortable she was because, when he finally broke the silence it was to say, "I'm sorry, I don't have a jacket to offer you."

"It's fine," she lied, absently wishing she could wrap one of her petticoats around her shoulders. She knew that wouldn't do, so she ignored the chill on her arms and sat down on a nearby bench. Not only did he follow, but he wrapped his arm around her, obviously in an attempt to keep her warm, which made it very difficult to begin the conversation the way she had intended, so for the time being she said nothing at all.

A few moments passed in silence before Charlie finally asked, "Is that better?" He leaned in toward her ear, the feeling of his warm breath on her skin sending a shiver down her spine.

Meg inhaled deeply before she nodded, still unable to speak. The feel of his arm around her and the close proximity to him in general were interfering with her reasoning skills again, and it was all she could do to regain her focus. Thoughts of little Ruth and Lizzy reminded her that she needed to take care of this the best way she could without upsetting Charlie to the point that he let Daniel go from his job.

As she continued to contemplate her word choice, he pulled her even closer, and she found herself twining her arms around him as well, her head on his shoulder. "Was there something specific you wanted to talk to me about?" he asked after another long moment of silence.

"Yes," she said quietly without looking up. He was twirling his fingers absently through the ends of her hair now, and she had to take another deep breath. Finally, she said, "I'm not exactly sure what, if anything, you had in mind, but... I don't know how this can work."

He said nothing for a moment, didn't shift his position, or pull his hand away from her golden locks. Meg thought for a moment perhaps she had misinterpreted his affection for her; maybe his silence was evidence that he was not looking for any sort of a relationship at all. However, eventually, he replied, "It seems to be working now."

His answer came as a relief to her, an indication that his feelings for her seemed to be in line with those she was clearly developing for him. She couldn't argue with his response either, and yet, she realized he had no idea why his choice in words—it *seemed* to be working—fit the situation so perfectly. After a moment, and a sigh of frustration, she continued. "But... you're you. And I'm, well, I don't even know who I am anymore... not really." She didn't dare look at him when she said those words, choosing instead to concentrate on the endless shadow beyond the distant railing that was the Atlantic Ocean.

Running his fingertips along her cheek, as if inviting her to look up at him, Charlie laughed and said, "You're Aunty Meg."

She could feel the warmth from his lips hovering just above her brow and knew if she tipped her face up just then, he would most certainly kiss her. While she wanted that more than anything, she fought it. She needed to press on in her resolve to tell him the truth. Charlie didn't seem satisfied with that response, so, he kissed the top of her head instead, which from Meg's interpretation was somehow almost as perfect, and the feel of his warm lips against her crown left her breathless.

Once again, thoughts of the girls drew her back to reality and gave her strength. She began to pull away from his embrace. "Oh, Charlie," she said as she took his arm from behind her back and brought it around to his lap, though she did not release his hand as she did so. "You couldn't possibly understand all of the reasons why... you don't deserve me."

His eyebrows shot up, and she realized she had misspoken—or at least he had misunderstood what she had been attempting to say. Before she could clarify, however, he said, "I would agree with that statement. I don't deserve you. Although, I must admit I am a little surprised to hear you say it...."

"No, that's not what I meant," she said, shaking her head in an attempt to unmuddy her thoughts. "I meant, you deserve BETTER than me. Not that you are not good enough for me. Obviously, you're far too good for me...."

"I disagree," he interrupted, a relieved look on his face as he was obviously holding back laughter at his own misunderstanding. "Just because you're a Third Class passenger and I'm a First Class passenger, that doesn't make me any better than you. In a lot of ways, it makes me far worse."

Meg's forehead furrowed in confusion. "What? No. I'm not sure I understand what could possibly be so humorous," she insisted, seeing the amusement playing in the corners of his eyes. "Charlie, I'm serious. There are so many things that you don't understand—important things."

Charlie did his best to stifle his laughter, and with both of her hands in his, he pulled her closer, saying, "I'm sorry. I'm not laughing at you. I promise. Just listen, Meg, whatever it is that makes you think you're not good enough for me, it doesn't matter. You're wrong."

She shifted her position again, pulling back a bit and turning to face him even more. "No, Charlie. That's just it. Don't you wonder why I won't tell you my last name? Or who I was before I got on this boat? Doesn't it bother you at all that I won't answer any of your questions about my family or my employment?"

While his tone was certainly more serious now, he shrugged in answer to her questions. "Those inquiries haven't come from me, Meg. They've come from Jonathan. From my perspective, it doesn't matter," he replied. Seeing the frustrated expression still on her face, he took a different approach. "You're not a murderer, are you?"

Meg's forehead furrowed as she attempted to understand this new line of questioning. "No," she admitted.

"Or a thief?" he continued.

She shook her head slowly from side to side.

"An arsonist?"

"No, but..."

"Then it doesn't matter, Meg. Whoever you were before you got on this boat is inconsequential. I know who you are now, and I find you most intriguing. And you can't tell me you don't feel the same way."

"I do Charlie, but..."

Before she could finish, he leaned forward, and placing one hand behind her head, he pulled her toward him. She attempted to fight him for only a split second, but that's all it took for her willpower to dissipate, and when he pressed his lips against hers, she suddenly felt as if she was floating. His lips were soft and warm, despite the cold night air, and when he began to pull away in an attempt to continue the conversation, she leaned in closer, her hand shooting up to the back of his neck, pulling him in. She could feel his smile at her enthusiasm, and when he pressed her to part her lips, she did, welcoming him into her mouth. Though she was confused by her own behavior--a moment ago, she had been pushing him away and now, she simply could not get enough of him—she was either unwilling or unable to control her desire for him any longer.

After a few seconds, clarity hit her again, and she started to pull back, realizing the seriousness of her actions. But this time he pulled her in closer for another kiss, his hand cupping her jaw, his thumb caressing her cheek, and she surrendered to him once again, their tongues intertwining.

Eventually, Meg began to feel her lungs burning and reluctantly pulled away. When Charlie finally released her, his face a fraction of an inch from hers, he said quietly, "You were saying?"

She was caught in those eyes, peering into his very soul, unsure how it was that when he looked into her own eyes, he couldn't see her for exactly who she was as well. If he could, none of this would be happening. After a moment, she found the words. Dropping her gaze and drawing her hands into her lap, she said quietly, "Just promise me, Charlie, when all of this comes undone, you won't hold any of it against Kelly and Daniel."

Charlie was obviously caught off-guard. He leaned back a bit, his eyebrows creasing. "Is that what you're worried about? That I'll get angry at you and change my mind about hiring Daniel? I would never...." He paused for a moment, as if contemplating in which direction he wanted to continue the conversation. Finally, he shrugged his shoulders and said, "It doesn't matter. I'm not even going to ask you to tell me your secrets, Meg. I don't want to know."

"But you need to know..."

"We all have pasts." He was lightly stroking her back, catching the tail ends of her curls as he did so, his eyes fading a bit as if ghostly memories had invaded his thoughts. Momentarily, he continued. "Hell, I was engaged to be married just a few days ago, you know."

Nodding with conviction, she assured him, "I do know. And there are things about me you need to know..."

"Meg, I'm not asking," he repeated, placing both hands on either side of her face. "Why won't you believe me when I say I just want to be with you?"

She realized then, as she studied his piercing green eyes, that short of blurting out her real name, there was no way she could gently reveal her true identity to him. And if he didn't give her the opportunity to explain everything the way she knew she needed to, she would lose him for certain. Though she knew it was completely and utterly selfish of her to even contemplate attempting to keep him for her own despite her recent transgressions, a life without him at this juncture was quickly becoming inconceivable.

Taking a deep breath, she placed her hands on top of his, pulling them away from her face but keeping hold of them. "Fine," she said quietly. "If you don't want to know, then I won't tell you."

"Good," he said, smiling. "Now, let's get you inside before you freeze." He leaned in and kissed her softly on the forehead before standing and pulling her to her feet. Taking her right hand in his left, he led her toward the stairwell to her deck, and added nonchalantly, "Oh, and I would be greatly honored if you would accompany me to dinner tomorrow night."

Meg froze, pulling him back to her as she did so. "What was that?" she asked.

"I said, I'd appreciate it if you'd join me for dinner tomorrow night. I have a friend who will help make sure you have a suitable gown. It'll be ... fun."

"You expect me to eat dinner with... Madeline Astor, and ... Lady Duff Gordon?" she inquired, sheer terror in her eyes.

Charlie shrugged, staring at her quizzically. He had expected excitement, not trepidation. "Well, those particular people don't sit at the same table, but people like them," he admitted. Still puzzling over her disposition, he continued, "Meg, darling, you are just as polished and beautiful as any of the women in the Banquet Hall, I assure you. You have nothing to worry about."

"But... I'm Third Class...."

"They won't know it unless we tell them. And I don't mind telling them, but of course I won't, unless you want me to."

"It's just... you don't..."

"Come on, sweetheart. It's cold out here," Charlie said, pulling her along. "You need not worry about it right now. It will be just fine."

She let him lead her inside, attempting to come to terms with what was inevitably about to happen. At least he'd promised to let Daniel keep his employment. That was the most important thing. Tomorrow, she'd show up to dinner, Madeline Astor or Lucy Duff Gordon, possibly the Strauses, would recognize her, she'd find a way for him to save face, and then he'd probably throw her overboard, a fate she would so very much deserve.

When they reached her door, she realized he was going to kiss her again, and she was going to let him, because this was likely the last time it would ever happen. She would stand there in her borrowed dress, outside a Steerage cabin aboard the grandest ship in the world, and let her fiancé of three years kiss her for only the second time, while he still had no idea that she was a lying, cheating, corrupted whore. Because that's what people like Mary Margaret Westmoreland did.

When she finally returned her attention to the gentleman before her, he was standing very close to her, his green eyes smiling at her, despite the terror she was only barely managing to hold back. "Thank you for asking me to dance," he said quietly, smiling down at her as he brushed her hair behind her shoulders and then wrapped his hands around her waist.

She placed her hands on his chest and managed to return his smile. "Thank you for... everything else," she replied.

"Please don't worry about tomorrow night," he assured her, leaning in. "It will be an occasion to remember."

She could certainly agree with that. With a loud sigh, she nodded, and acquiesced with a reserved, "All right." His face was hovering just in front of hers now, and with every fiber of her being, she wanted to believe that he was right—that it would be just fine. She didn't wait for him to kiss her. Instead, she rose up on her tiptoes and found his lips with hers, sliding her hand up to his jawline to press his lips apart. He returned her kiss just as hungrily, possibly a bit surprised at her spontaneity, and he gently forced her back against the wall, his body pressed against hers. His very presence seemed to push all of the unwelcome, ugly thoughts out of her mind, and Meg felt herself responding to him in a way that she never would have thought possible. Just as she began to lose herself entirely, the sound of footsteps on the stairs caught his attention, and he seemed to remember himself, pulling away from her. With a sharp exhale, Meg released him, aware that her lips were still quivering as she did so.

Green eyes dancing, he whispered, "I'll see you tomorrow," and squeezed her hand one last time as he turned to go, glancing back at her over his broad shoulders, with a crooked grin, a few steps down the dimly lit hall.

She watched him disappear down the corridor, her body still trembling. Once he was out of sight, she carefully opened the cabin door and slipped inside, pressing her back to the door and pausing to regain her composure before she ran her hands through her blonde tresses, attempting to bring herself back to reality.

Eventually, she crossed over to her bed, taking her boots off, and finding her sleeping gown. She was certain everyone else was asleep, including Daniel, who happened to be facing away from her, but she discretely changed before climbing into bed. She knew if there was one chance in her lifetime to go to sleep without nightmares, this was her opportunity. Her past had haunted her for over a decade; her future was brewing with dark clouds. But for right now, in this moment, at long last, she was finally truly happy.

❧

JONATHAN WAS WAITING for him when he arrived, which was no surprise. He had not been able to wipe the smile off of his face the entire stroll back to his own stateroom, and now that he was sitting across from his friend, absently thumping his hands on the arms of his chair, his attitude had not changed.

"It went well, then?" Jonathan asked. He had offered Charlie a brandy, which had been refused, a sure sign that something was different.

"She's... incredible," he replied with a deep sigh.

Jonathan nodded, running a hand through his dark, slightly graying, hair. "Any further information?"

"Nope."

"A last name?"

"Nope."

"Occupation, perhaps?"

"No. And it doesn't matter," Charlie replied sharply. "Whoever she is, wherever she came from, she's here now, and that's all that I care about."

Jonathan let out a very different sort of sigh, one of frustration. "All right then, if you insist." Then, after a moment, he asked, "Did you...?"

Charlie looked at him incredulously. "Jonathan, please! She's a lady!"

"Is she now?" he asked. "I mean, how would one know, what with no last name and all?"

"One can tell a lady without knowing her last name. Or her station, I might add," Charlie retorted, crossing his arm against his chest.

"You're right," Jonathan responded, rolling his eyes. "I'm sure Aunty Meg is completely virtuous, no doubt."

"What is that supposed to mean?" Charlie asked, slamming his hands down against the chair arms. Shaking his head in shock, he continued. "She very well might be. Not that it matters. I told you, I don't care."

"All right, then," Jonathan said, standing, the threat of losing his cool completely bubbling near the surface. "I'm going to leave you. But if the Charlie I know should happen to show up, please tell him I'll be calling on him for breakfast in the morning."

Charlie crossed his arms again defiantly and looked at his friend rather sharply before saying, "You just don't understand."

"You're right, I don't understand," Jonathan admitted, turning back to face his friend. After a moment, and a sigh of both frustration and contemplation, he continued, "But then, maybe I don't need to. Maybe the only thing that matters is that she makes you happy. God knows you deserve it after everything you've been through."

"I do deserve it," Charlie agreed, his green eyes locked on something in the distance, his head nodding slightly with each word. As if regaining his composure, he then turned to look at his valet and added, "Oh, and she's going to accompany me to dinner tomorrow evening, for your information."

Jonathan's eyes widened in surprise, his mouth hanging open for a moment before he managed to ask, "Oh, really?"

"Yes, it was Molly Brown's idea, but I dare I say, I think it's a good one."

"And is Mrs. Brown going to help Miss Meg dress?" Jonathan probed.

"She is, actually," Charlie confirmed.

Placing his hands on his hips, Jonathan replied, "Well, it should be quite interesting to see the reaction of the rest of the socialites when you show up with this unknown woman on your arm."

"I suppose so," Charlie agreed, absently running his hand through his hair. "I'm just happy to have the opportunity to spend more time with her and let her see a glimpse of my world—ridiculous as it may be. She needs to know what she's getting herself in to."

Once again, Jonathan paused. "You know, Charlie, this sounds quite serious. Let us not forget, your father still thinks you're engaged to Miss Westmoreland."

"Oh, I haven't forgotten."

Nodding, as if to say he was certain that was true, Jonathan continued. "And what do you think your father is going to say when he meets Miss Meg?"

"I don't care."

"Fair enough."

CHAPTER 10

M eg had slept in the morning of April 13 well past the last call for breakfast. Kelly had also slumbered on for quite some time, though hungry children were able to poke and prod enough to finally get her out of bed in time for a morning meal. While Daniel was still in obvious pain, he had managed to leave the small cabin with the boisterous little lass, her sister, and their overly tired mother, leaving Meg to roll back over and continue what could no doubt be considered the best sleep of her life.

There had been no nightmares, despite the fact that she knew she'd be walking in to a real live one later that evening, and she had dreamt only of Charlie and the life they would have had together had she only done the right thing in the first place. When she finally pulled herself from bed and dressed just before noon, she did so with an air of solemnity. Regardless of how she handled herself this evening—walking into the hornet's nest without giving him fair warning, or showing up and praying for the best—he would end the night knowing precisely who she was. Whether or not he would let her explain her reasoning was unclear for now, but that was the one prayer on her tongue as she set about her morning. Unfortunately, she knew God didn't owe her anything.

She was able to catch up with the rest of her family in the Third Class Dining Lounge for lunch. They had just taken seats when she arrived, and Ruth in particular was overjoyed to see her. "Aunty Meg! Did you dance with Uncle Charlie at the party last night?" she asked in her melodic voice.

Meg glanced at Kelly who shrugged, clearly having told her nothing. "Why do you ask?" she asked, placing a napkin on her lap.

"Because he's a prince, and you're a princess. That's who is supposed to dance together at the ball!" she exclaimed swinging her doll in the air.

"Well, it wasn't a ball," Meg reminded her. "It was just a party."

"But Dolly New Eyes says it's the same!" Ruth insisted.

Dolly New Eyes had gotten her name when Daddy had to replace the originals with marbles last year. The doll had been Meg's when she was a girl, but now she was Ruth's fondest friend, and she was rather happy to see her out and about aboard the *Titanic*. "Dolly New Eyes knows a lot about such things, then?" Meg asked.

"Yes, she does," Ruth nodded.

"All right, then. I suppose they are similar. And yes, I did dance with Uncle Charlie last night. But, sweetheart, you mustn't think that Aunt Meg and Uncle Charlie are a prince and princess who will get married someday. That can't happen," she explained, catching Kelly's and then Daniel's eyes.

"Why not?" Ruth pressed on, a puckered expression on her face.

"Because Aunt Meg isn't a real princess, and Uncle Charlie must marry a real princess who does royal things and lives in a castle with servants...."

"But you used to have servants and live in a grand house. Mummy..."

"Not any more, darlin'," Kelly exclaimed. "Aunty Meg is just like us now. She will have a job and wear clothes like ours. She will marry a fine, hardworking man like your father."

The disappointment on Ruth's face was obvious and unsettling. "But Aunt Meg has to be a princess. You can't stop being a princess. No, you'll see. You're wrong, Mummy. Aunt Meg, Uncle Charlie is your prince. You'll marry him and live in a grand house in New Yowk. You'll see."

"All right, sweetheart," Meg said, offering a small smile. Then, in an attempt to change the subject, she offered, "Now, what are we having for supper?"

⌘

"OH, this is going to be so good!" Molly Brown exclaimed as she sat across from Charlie at a secluded lunch table in the First Class *a la carte* dining room. "I am so glad that your friend agreed to come! It's sort of like plannin' a weddin'..."

"Let's not get ahead of ourselves," Charlie cut her off.

"Oh, no, that's not what I meant. Don't worry. I ain't gettin' ya hitched just yet. I mean, everything's got to be just perfect, you know? Right dress, right shoes, right timing. That sort of thing," she explained taking a bite of Waldorf salad. "What's she look like?"

"She's beautiful," he replied, a starry-eyed glaze forming over his handsome face.

Molly giggled. "That ain't very helpful there, Romeo. I mean, is she short or tall? Thin or curvy? Light hair or dark hair?"

"Oh, right," Charlie said, dragging himself back to reality. "She's sort of tall, I guess, for a woman. Taller than you. She's ... fit I guess you could say. Certainly not pudgy but not scrawny either. She has beautiful blonde locks, and most of the time she wears them down... and beautiful blue eyes."

"Wears her hair down? Guess a lot of them Third Class passengers do that. You sure she's old enough for you, stretch?"

"I'm sure she's old enough, yes," he replied, although it was true that he had no idea of her age, not really.

"All right. I'll probably have to borrow a dress from Lucy," she muttered almost to herself. Lady Duff Gordon was a well-known fashion designer, so chances were she would have some appropriate attire to choose from. "Shoes might be tricky. Did you happen to notice whether or not she had big feet?"

Charlie chuckled. "We spent quite some time dancing last night—and not very well. Luckily for me her feet are rather small." Memories of the night before sent him off again, and Molly shook her head at him, a small smile on her face. Eventually, he noticed her stare and asked, "What? Whatever are you laughing about?"

"Could you try to stay with me until we get this figured out?" she prodded, chuckling quietly.

"I'm sorry... it's just... she's so.... Wait until you meet her Molly," he finally concluded.

"Can't wait," Molly assured him. "Dinner starts at six sharp. It'll take at least two hours to get her ready. Can you send your man-servant—what's his name, Jonathan?—to fetch her and bring her to me around four o'clock?"

"It takes two hours for you to get ready for dinner?" Charlie asked in shock. "What in the world takes so long?"

"A lady never reveals her beauty secrets," Molly replied, a gleam in her eye. Of course, there was no need to explain she had factored in a bit of time for emergencies—dress not fitting, unsightly Third Class nails, that sort of thing. "Don't cha worry, Charlie. I'll get her to you all spiffy and on time for the ball."

He knew her words were meant only as a metaphor, but he couldn't help think of the last time he was waiting for a girl at a ball—one that would never show. He pushed those thoughts aside. If Mary Margaret had attended the ball that night, he would have never met Meg.

"By the way, what's this girl's name anyhow?" Molly asked.

"Meg," he replied, the dreamy expression back.

"Meg? Huh, another Margaret. My kinda gal," she mumbled before taking a bite of roasted duck.

"What's that?" Charlie asked, not quite sure he understood.

"Margaret—Meg is usually short for Margaret. Molly is short for Margaret. We have the same name," she explained after a few moments of chewing.

"Right," he replied. "I guess I hadn't thought about it."

"What's her last name?"

There was that question again. "I don't know," he admitted.

Molly's eyebrows arched. "You don't know? How's that? Never asked?"

"No, it's not that. It just... it doesn't matter. She's just Meg. And that's all she needs to be."

"Well, alrighty then."

CHAPTER 11

"Do you think he'll send someone to fetch you?" Kelly asked as she and Meg made their way along the Boat Deck. Ruth was walking between them, carrying Dolly New Eyes, her father having returned to the cabin with Lizzy after lunch.

"I suppose so," Meg replied. "Dinner starts at six, so I should probably head back down around three or so, just to be sure I'm there when I'm called on."

Kelly nodded. "I'm sure Jonathan will get that job. He's a bit... odd, don't you think?"

Meg considered the statement for a moment. "Odd? How so? I hadn't really noticed."

Kelly glanced down at her daughter for a moment to see if she were listening before she continued. "I don't know. He just seems like a bit of a confirmed bachelor to me, that's all."

"How's that?" Meg asked, not sure she followed.

Kelly sighed, absently patting Ruth on the head. "Come on now, Meg. Don't play daft. You know." She continued in a harsh whisper. "A Mary-Jane."

"Oh," Meg said, finally catching on. "I don't... think so. Why would you think that?"

"I don't know," Kelly shrugged. "Maybe not. Perhaps I shouldn't have said anything. He just seems to treat Charlie a little bit like... he wishes.... It doesn't matter."

Meg's eyebrows were furrowed. "Surely you aren't implying that Charlie...."

"Oh, heavens no," Kelly assured her, shooting her hand out to squeeze Meg's arm. "Not at all. Forget it. I shouldn't have said anything."

"All right," Meg said still wondering what Kelly's concern was. "Well, if you're afraid that Jonathan is leery of me, afraid I'm going to break Charlie's heart, then I think you're right. And so is he. Again. How can I keep breaking the same man's heart over and over again?" Her voice had trailed off at the end, and she found herself choking back tears.

"About that," Kelly said as they stepped past an older couple huddled together on a bench, "I was thinking, are you sure you have to tell him? What if no one recognizes you?"

"They will most certainly recognize me, Kelly. I've gone to several events with many of these people over the years—recent years—and unlike Charlie who hasn't received an updated photograph of me since I was about twelve, they know precisely what I look like," Meg assured her.

"All right. So let's say they don't notice. Maybe you don't have to tell him, not yet. Wait until he gets to know you a little better and can see you for who you really are. Then, maybe once he finds out you're actually already engaged, he'll be happy."

"Oh, Kelly, I wish it were that simple. But you need to realize— despite your biased position—it was the 'real me' that did all of these horrible things in the first place." She watched Kelly's eyes dart down to Ruth, as if to indicate Meg should be careful of her words. She understood and spoke carefully as she continued. "We would not be in this situation if I hadn't l-i-e-d, and c-h-e-a-t-e-d. Remember that. He deserves to know the truth. I should have told him last night, but he refused to hear what I had to say. I'm sure, after tonight, there's no way to avoid it."

"I do wish it didn't have to be so," Kelly said, locking her arm with Meg's. "You both seem so happy when you're together."

"I know," Meg agreed, resting her head on Kelly's shoulder. "Who would have thought my mother was right after all?"

"It wasn't your mother," Kelly reminded her. "This was your father's idea."

Meg leaned up in contemplation. "True, but all these years it's been my mother and her greed that has pressed the issue."

"Yes, but your father chose Charlie to take care of you. He knew he was a good man from a good family. That has nothing to do with your mother or her hopes of gainin' financial security through your marriage."

"Oh, God, Kelly," Meg said, stopping and turning to face her friend. "I hadn't thought about it that way. I mean, of course I knew my father had made the arrangements. But it never crossed my mind to attribute this lack of choice to my father and his wisdom. I always just thought of the whole thing as another of my mother's schemes." She ran her hand through her long blond tresses. "If I had been considering the entire situation from that perspective all along, perhaps we wouldn't be in this situation now."

Kelly clenched her friend's hand. "In life, there are a lot of chances for regret and never enough opportunities for acceptance. That's why I think you should take every chance to mend this, if you can, before you completely give up on Charlie. Don't forget, Meg, I know you. Better than anyone. And despite what you think, you do deserve to be happy. And so does he. If you can salvage a life together out of this, do it. Life is too short to wonder what might have been."

Meg pulled Kelly into her arms and squeezed her tightly. "Oh, Kelly, what would I ever do without you?"

"Don't worry—you'll never have to find out." After another moment, she pulled back sharply and began looking around in earnest. "Where's Ruth?"

Meg laughed. "She's right there," she said, pointing over at one of the lifeboats where Ruth was having a discussion with her doll.

"Jesus, Mary, and Joseph that girl is going to give me heart failure,"

Kelly muttered as she crossed the few steps to where her daughter was playing.

"And then, we'll get inside the little boat and sail to a new boat. And everything will be just fine," she was explaining to Dolly New Eyes.

"What are you doin' my wee lass?" Kelly asked, running her hand through Ruth's hair.

"I didn't run away," Ruth assured her, looking up with wide eyes.

"No, I know you didn't darlin'. Mummy could see you. I just panicked a bit, that's all," Kelly explained.

"I was just telling Dolly New Eyes she didn't need to be scared when we get in the lifeboats, you see?" Ruth said matter-of-factly.

"Oh, sweetie, we won't be gettin' in the lifeboats. Those are just for emergencies," her mother replied, dropping down to her knees.

"I know," Ruth admitted, shaking her head. "I told Dolly not to worry, that I will always take care of her, and we'll be safe. And Mummy, Daddy, Baby Lizzy, Aunt Meg, Uncle Charlie, and Mr. Jonaffin will be safe, too. We'll all be together on the new boat."

"You have quite the imagination, love," Meg said patting her on the head. "This is the strongest boat they ever built. Nothing can sink it."

"God can sink it," Ruth reminded her, a hauntingly stern expression in her eyes as she reached out to take Meg's hand. And then, just as quickly as it had come, the peculiar countenance passed, and with a smile, she asked, "Can we go see Daddy now? I want to check if his arm is better."

Meg was still puzzling over the oddness of Ruth's behavior so she said nothing. Rather, Kelly replied, "Yes, of course," as she patted her daughter's head. "Thank you for staying with Mummy and Aunty Meg today, Ruthy. You've been an extra good girl."

"You're welcome, Mummy," Ruth said smiling innocently. "Dolly New Eyes was a good girl to stay with us, too," she added.

"Yes, she was," Kelly assured her as they made their way back below deck, giving no more consideration to Ruth's fortuitous remarks.

⚜

IT WAS PROMPTLY four o'clock when a knock on the door brought Meg to her feet, the butterflies in her stomach mimicking Josephine on her flying trapeze. She pulled the door open to find Jonathan, just as she had expected. "Good afternoon," she said, managing a smile.

"Miss Meg," he said, tipping his bowler hat. "I've come to escort you to Mrs. Molly Brown's stateroom, if you're ready."

"Mr. Jonaffin!" Ruth said, tumbling down from the top bunk where she had been playing and bounding across the room, flinging herself at his knees. "I missed you! Where's Uncle Charlie?"

Scooping her up, he replied, "He's getting ready for dinner with Aunty Meg."

"Oh!" She leaned over and whispered sharply into his ear, "She doesn't remember she's a princess. Will you help her remember?"

"Yes, sweetheart, I'll help her," he assured her.

She smiled sweetly as he sat her back down, and Kelly stepped over behind her. "Tell Mr. Jonathan we'll see him later, darlin'. He has important things to do."

"Goodbye, Mr. Jonaffin!" she said waving.

"Goodbye Miss Ruth," he replied waving. "Are you ready then?" he asked, returning his attention to Meg.

"As ready as I shall ever be," she nodded.

"Then, let's go."

Meg waved goodbye to the family, catching Kelly's eyes for a moment before she stepped through the door, and as she was closing it behind her, the distinct sound of Ruth's voice followed them out into the hallway, asking, "Daddy, what's a Mary-Jane?"

Meg's face turned bright red, but she just kept right on walking, hoping that Jonathan did not hear the question, and that if he did he didn't associate its asking with any discussions about himself. Clearly, however, he had heard what the little one had asked and assumed his presence had prompted the inquiry. Meg could tell by the slight change in his disposition. Rather than attempt an explanation, an apology, or a weak joke about children's antics, she chose to ignore the incident entirely.

It took a while before Jonathan said anything at all, and in a way, Meg was almost thankful for Ruth's innocent, yet offensive, statement because it seemed to spare her at least a bit of idle chatter—or possibly intense conversation, as the case may be. Eventually, he asked, "How did you sleep last night after the festivities?"

"Well," she assured him. "Thank you for asking. And yourself?"

"Fine," he replied, nodding. "Did the girls let you sleep in a bit?"

"Kelly and Daniel took them to breakfast, and honestly, I slept well past noon," she admitted.

He guided her toward the stairwell that led to the First Class section of the boat, an area she would generally not be permitted to enter under normal circumstances were she not escorted by the valet of a First Class passenger. Jonathan was actually staying in Second Class, but he was free to move between the areas as needed so that he could provide the services his employer required. Steerage passengers were more limited in their permissions to travel freely about the vessel.

"You must be quite the conversationalist, Miss Meg," he probed as they continued to make their way to Mrs. Brown's room. "Charlie seems quite intrigued by you."

"Is that so?" she asked, unwilling to give him any information he hadn't earned.

"Indeed. I trust you had some time to catch up on each other's histories, that sort of thing, once you left the party?"

She smiled. "Mr. Lane, am I to presume that you haven't spoken to Charlie about the content of our discussion last night? Or that you were never able to track us down after we left the dance?"

He stopped for a moment, turning to look at her, before continuing. "Are you accusing me of eavesdropping?"

"Not at all. But you wouldn't be a very good valet if you weren't always one step ahead of your employer. Let's just say I am under the impression you are quite skilled at your trade, Mr. Lane."

He smirked at her. "You've started calling me Mr. Lane again, and yet I still have no idea what your surname is," he reminded her.

"And you probably know that I was more than willing to discuss it with Mr. Ashton last night, but he refused."

They paused in front of a stateroom door, and Meg assumed they had arrived at their destination. Before he knocked, Jonathan turned to her and said quietly, "Call me what you will, I only have Charlie's

best interest at heart. You're from Southampton. I'm sure you know—
he's been through enough. If this is a game, Miss Meg, you'd better
ensure yourself to be on the losing end, or I will take care of that for
you. Are we clear?"

"Crystal."

He nodded and smiling politely, he rapped on the door sharply
twice, and they waited briefly for it to open, an awkward silence
hanging between them.

When the door finally did open, it wasn't a servant girl, as
expected, but Mrs. Brown herself. "Well, here she is!" she exclaimed,
throwing the door open.

"Mrs. Margaret Brown this is... Meg," Jonathan said by way of
introduction.

"I know who she is, Jonathan," Molly said waving a dismissive hand
at him. "Better not be anybody else dropping their date off to get
gussied up, or we'll run out of time for sure. All right then, boy. You let
Charlie know she's in good hands, and we'll see him in a couple of
hours. Got it, slick?"

"Yes, madam," Jonathan replied, giving Meg one last pointed
stare before she entered the room, and Molly shut the door
behind her.

"Look at you!" Molly said, taking Meg by the arms and stretching
them out in front of her. "Charlie said you were beautiful, but I think
he may have understated. Wish I could say I used to have a figure like
yours, but that would be paintin' a pig and calling it Petunia," she
continued.

Meg wasn't quite used to her accent or her strange expressions, so
it took her a moment to understand exactly what she was saying. She
did catch the "Charlie said you were beautiful" part, which made
her blush.

"Turn around and let me have a look atcha," Molly insisted.

Meg felt rather odd but complied. "Mrs. Brown," she said as she
turned back to face the woman who was studying her as if she were
about to paint her portrait, "I need to speak to you before we get
started. It's a matter with quite a bit of urgency."

"I'm sure one of them dresses Lucy gave me oughtta do nicely,"

Molly muttered as if she hadn't heard Meg's comment. "Maybe the black one... or the red..."

"Lucy?" Meg repeated. "As in Lady Duff Gordon?"

"Oh, yes," Molly replied. "How handy is it to have a famous dress designer on board when you have a fashion emergency?"

Meg swallowed hard. If Lucy knew she were borrowing her dress, she'd definitely want to see her in it. And then she'd certainly let everyone know who she was, which could be quite embarrassing for Charlie. "Mrs. Brown..."

"Molly..."

"Molly, it's vitally important that we speak before this goes any further. Listen, I'm not who you think I am. Not who Charlie thinks I am. I need your help, or else this is going to be catastrophic for him, and I can't let that happen, not again."

She had Molly's attention then at last. "Christine, bring us some tea," she said to the servant girl waiting nearby. "Have a seat, honey," she continued gesturing to the sofa, her face showing concern and suspicion.

Meg complied, and Molly sat down at the other end of the couch, a considerable space between them. "Before I tell you who I really am, I would ask that you please let me explain how all of this came to be. When I'm finished, if you don't want to help me, I will completely understand. But please promise you will hear my story in its entirety before you toss me out."

Molly only nodded, her expression growing more and more skeptical as Meg continued.

Meg took a deep breath, still trying to determine where to begin. Finally, she said, "I tried to explain things to him last night, but he didn't want to hear it. I don't want you to think that I am intentionally telling you before I tell him. I truly tried—but he said nothing before *Titanic* matters. I disagree. I know he will, too, once he finds out."

"I agree—with you," Molly said nodding. "Go on."

"My name's not really Meg. I mean, it is... but it's not." She shook her head, attempting to clear her thoughts. After a deep breath, she tried again. "It's Mary Margaret."

There was a moment of silence as Molly either put the pieces together or came to grips with the revelation. Eventually, she simply asked, "Westmoreland?"

"Yes."

Molly's expression turned to anger, her lips pierced into a thin line. Just then, the servant girl returned with the tea, and Molly gestured for her to set it on the coffee table. "I reckon you've got a lot of explaining to do."

Again, Meg replied only, "Yes."

She reached for the teapot then, pouring her own though Christine attempted to step forward to do so. Molly gestured for her to leave the room, which she did, shutting the door behind her. "How do you take your tea, Miss Westmoreland?"

"Oh, no thank..."

"Two lumps of sugar or three?"

Meg swallowed hard again at the abrasive tone. "Two, please," she replied just above a whisper. She took the teacup, sipping it slowly before setting it back down. Molly was staring at her, waiting for an explanation, which she certainly deserved. "I don't know how much you're aware of..."

"Plenty."

"All right then. I hope you can understand; my intention was never to hurt Charlie. I was only trying to get back at my mother. To get free from my mother, actually. If anything, I thought he would be just as happy as I was to be free of the burden of an arranged marriage."

"Then you don't know Charlie very well do you?" Molly asked, taking a rather loud slurp of her beverage.

Meg let out an audible sigh before admitting, "No, I guess I didn't. Which is remarkable because he wrote me letter after letter over the years. Many of them, I'm afraid I didn't even read. I just placed them in a box in my closet. I just assumed he felt the same way I did—that this was a sham meant to make our parents happy, not us.

"Of course, I was wrong. I found that out pretty quickly... once I did what I did... skipped out on the ball. I overheard the conversation from my room between my mother and Charlie. She assured him I had every intent in going through with the marriage, and he said he had considered me his wife for so long, he wouldn't even know how to begin to look for another. I had no idea he had felt that way. And yet, even after hearing that, I still blamed him. I watched him leave that day, in the rain, from my bedroom window. I still had the opportunity to salvage our relationship. But I chose not to. Maybe, deep down inside, it was the realization that he really did want to be with me that helped me to see he deserves someone far better than I. You see, while I was in Southampton plotting my escape, he was in New York dreaming of some beautiful young woman, waiting for him, keeping herself only for him." She stopped for a moment, glancing at Molly, whose expression hadn't changed, and then trained her eyes on a spot on the carpet. "I wasn't able to do that." She glanced up again and seeing the shift in her expression, she realized Mrs. Brown thought she was saying she had always been a loose girl. She knew she would have to tell her the truth—the whole truth—if she was to salvage any respect at all. Before opening that other chapter, she continued with her point. "Charlie deserves to be with someone who is just as thoughtful and kindhearted as he is."

"Again, I agree." She took another sip and then asked, "So then, why are you here?"

"Because he needs to know the truth... why I did the things I did. That it wasn't his fault I ran away from him. That he didn't do anything wrong."

"Well, girl, at least one of us is headed to dinner soon, so if you're going to explain all of that to me, you best get to talkin'."

Meg took a deep breath and steadied herself to say a phrase she had only repeated to those the very closest to her over the last several years. "My Uncle Bertram began molesting me when I was seven years old." Molly gasped, but Meg didn't wait. She needed to power on or else she would lose her courage to speak. "I thought it was my fault, that I'd done something wrong. I tried to tell my mother, but she punished me severely for saying such things about my uncle. Anytime I tried to reach out to anyone, that person would end up hurt... or worse. I even contemplated telling Charlie, but my mother read everything I wrote to him. I had no one to turn to, and despite the fact that marrying him would provide a means of escape, all my mother ever talked about was marrying into the Ashton family so we could live by their means. My mother is a greedy, vindictive woman. I have no idea how someone as kindhearted and loving as my father could have ever seen her fit to marry. Perhaps she fooled him into thinking she was worthy of his love solely so she could have his money as well. Anyway, despite wanting out of my situation, I began to see Charlie as part of the problem—that if I married him, my mother and uncle would win. I failed to see the loving man my father had chosen for me, focusing only on the financial gain my mother so desperately longed for.

"And then one day, I was sitting outside by the carriage house weeping over my situation, and one of my childhood friends, Ezra, approached me, asking what was wrong. I poured my heart out to him, and for the first time in a long time, I felt that someone was listening to me—that he cared about me. He promised me he would find a way to get me out of my uncle's clutches. Over time, we began to talk about running away. He said he loved me, and I believed him.

"When Charlie arrived, and I was to meet him at Alise's ball, I knew my time was up. I met Ezra in the carriage house that night instead of going to the ball, begging him to run away with me right that very moment. I had saved enough money to book passage on the *Titanic*. I planned to take my lady, Kelly, and her family along, and they were ready to leave at a moment's notice as well. But Ezra insisted I prove my love to him first. So, I did. While Charlie was at the ball, waiting for me, I was in the carriage house with Ezra.

"When we were finished, I urged him to leave with me at once, but he said he couldn't just then, that he had to stay until the next day, to say goodbye to his father. I explained that, if my mother realized I hadn't attended the ball, she would be furious. I wasn't exactly sure what she'd do to me, but I knew it would be horrific. He assured me that he would stand beside me, that he wouldn't let anything happen to me.

"Of course, my mother knew immediately that I had skipped out on Charlie and the ball. The next morning, she summoned me to the parlor. My uncle was there as well. I knew that Ezra was in the adjoining room, and his presence gave me strength. I looked my mother in the eye, and I told her that I wouldn't marry Charlie, that I was in love with Ezra, and that we were planning a life together. I was waiting for him to come in, to rescue me. When my mother struck me the first time, I thought for sure he would storm in then. I yelled for him, but he was silent. She slapped me across the face repeatedly until I was sure my eyeballs would come out of their sockets. Then, the unthinkable happened." Tears began to well up in Meg's eyes as she relived the events of only a few days ago. She had never told this part of the story to anyone, not even Kelly. "My uncle grabbed me by my arm, tossed me over his shoulder and dragged me up the stairs. I realized what was happening almost instantly, and I tried to fight him, but in that position, there was little I could do. I screamed for Ezra—for anyone. But my lady, Kelly, she wasn't home, and no one else would help. No one. Not even Ezra.

"He took me to my room, threw me on the bed, and ... he forced himself upon me... the whole time calling me a whore, telling me no one would have me now, that I was completely spoilt. By the time he was done, I was crying so hard, I was even begging for my mother to help. She stood in the doorway and watched him pull up his pants, never saying a word to me until he was gone. Then, she looked me in the eye and said, 'I hope you're happy. You've ruined everything.' And then she slammed the door, locking it behind her.

"A few hours later, I heard Charlie downstairs, and in my distress, I lumped him in with the rest of them, blaming him for bringing this misery upon me. Of course, I realize now, if I had only spoken up, he is the one person who would have charged up those stairs to save me. But by then, I realized my uncle was right. I was no longer worthy of becoming Mrs. Charles Ashton.

"The next morning, Kelly returned to duty. When she arrived in my room, I was ready to go. It was April 9, and I knew, if we were to book passage aboard the *Titanic*, we needed to do so immediately. Despite his unwillingness to help me the day before, I was still dreaming of a life with Ezra. At that point, it seemed as if he were my only hope. It wasn't until Kelly explained to me that Ezra had left the night before, whisking away the house maid, Charlotte, that I understood I had been living a complete and utter farce. Ezra didn't love me—he'd only been using me. When he found out he could be in danger at the hand of my uncle or mum, he disappeared. I was determined at that point to escape myself. I waited until my mother and uncle were preoccupied and we lit off to a hotel for the night while Kelly's husband, Daniel, booked passage aboard the RMS *Titanic*."

Molly had been silent the entire time, except for a sigh or a gasp here and there, the swatting away of a tear from time to time. At last she asked, "And how did you happen to meet Charlie once you were aboard?"

For the first time in a while, Meg began to smile, remembering that happy occurrence. "It was Ruth," she replied, "my niece. Well, Kelly's daughter. She ran to him on the promenade, took to him immediately, referring to him as Uncle Charlie. It was as if she somehow knew he was meant to be in her life... had been... had been meant to be in her life."

"And he didn't recognize you?"

"No," she confirmed. "I thought he would. I recognized him immediately, of course. But my mother wasn't very good about sending photographs, and I try to stay out of Southampton's high society newspapers the best I can. I tried to avoid him, but every time I turned around there he was. And the more I got to know him, the more I realized how very wrong I was about him. He's a wonderful person, Mrs. Brown—not at all the arrogant, greedy, narcissistic millionaire I had always made him out to be." Molly was nodding in agreement. Meg paused for a moment. "Anyway, I know he can do far better than the likes of me, but for some reason, despite my insistence that we should not be together, here I am.... Charlie doesn't deserve to have his heart broken again, especially not by me. But if I show up in that dining hall, plenty of people are going to recognize me. And if I don't show up, well, that's going to break his heart, too."

Molly set her teacup on the saucer before her on the coffee table and slid across the sofa so that she was right next to Meg. Without saying a word, she wrapped her arms around the young girl, pulling her head to her shoulder. Meg thought she had gotten over her tears, but at Molly's gentle touch, she began to sob, and the mothering instinct took over, as she smoothed her hair and rocked her gently. After a few moments, Meg began to regain her composure, and Molly pulled her head up to look her in the eyes. "Meg, darlin', you can't hold yourself responsible for the horrible things that happened to you. People think because of our station we don't suffer the inhumanities the rest of the world endures. They're wrong. You're a victim here, too, honey. Your uncle oughta have his testicles chewed off by fire ants, and your mother deserves a lashing, too. Did you make some mistakes along the way? Course you did. Ain't nobody perfect. But all of this is a direct result of what that bastard did to you. And I am not about to sit here and watch him ruin your last chance at findin' happiness with Charlie."

Meg's eyes widened. "You'll help me then?" she asked, shocked.

"Damn right I'll help you," Molly replied. "Now come on, girl, let's get you dressed."

CHAPTER 12

They were late. Not as late as Meg had anticipated considering they hadn't even begun dressing until almost five o'clock, but slightly late nonetheless. Dressed in a velvet and silk Chantilly lace gown in black, with a small train, square neckline, and netted sleeves, featuring red floral embroidered tulle at the waistline and splendid bead work, her hair in a low chignon with matching beads interlaced, a diamond necklace she had borrowed from Molly featuring a *flor de lis* and matching diamond earrings, and red, satin, beaded slippers, Meg was finally beginning to feel like herself again.

She had briefed Molly on precisely who she felt she needed to avoid, as best she could tell, and they had come up with a plan for what to do should her cover be blown. Arriving a bit late actually helped in some ways, as most of the diners were already seated before she entered, giving less of an opportunity for them to linger at the bottom of the grand staircase. In fact, as Meg began to descend the opulent structure, there was only one person paying her any attention at all, and the sight of him took her breath away.

He was leaning against the newel post next to an illuminated cherub, dressed in full tailcoats, smiling up at her, his green eyes sparkling, and as she approached, she realized she was holding her breath. "Meg, you are exquisite," he said, taking her gloved hand in his and kissing it gently.

"Thank you," she replied, smiling at him, almost giddily. "You look... amazing, as well," she stammered.

Nodding, he replied, "Thank you," and offered her his arm. Molly was stepping around them, planning to run interference should it be necessary, and he greeted her as well, saying, "Thank you ever so much for your help."

"My pleasure, Charlie," she said, patting him on the arm as she stepped away. "That Meg's a fine gal."

"Yes, she is," he agreed, staring at her intently. "Yes, she is."

As he led her to the assigned dining table (an extra place had been set for her) she glanced about the room, looking for potential threats. She saw Madeline Astor across the room, her back to the table they were headed toward. She did not see the Strauses anywhere. And while it looked like Lady Duff Gordon would have a nice view of where Meg and Charlie would be sitting, Meg would have her back turned to her dress designer, which could cause potential problems, except for Molly was seated where she could keep an eye out if Lucy were to approach their table.

Meg was relieved that she did not recognize anyone at the table. A few of the names seemed familiar as Charlie introduced her, but there was no one present she had ever met before. Of course, they were all curious as to who she was and where she had come from. Charlie simply explained, "She's the aunt of the young lady who almost fell overboard yesterday," to which Molly added, "You mean the girl you saved," and that seemed sufficient for most who asked her several questions, many of which had to do with health of the girl's father and the accommodations in Steerage.

Each time Meg glanced in Charlie's direction—which was frequent —he was beaming at her. "Whatever is the matter with you?" she finally asked, leaning in so that others might not overhear.

"Nothing in the world," he replied. "I just can't take my eyes off of you. I told you, you would fit right in. Your manners are impeccable. You even know which fork to use."

"I wasn't raised in a barn, you know," she jested. Still, she thought, perhaps, she should seem a little less polished so that her familiarity wasn't so obvious.

"Nevertheless, I'm quite impressed. Your mother must be quite some woman to teach you such proper etiquette and how to dance," he replied as the waiter removed their third course plates.

"Oh, she's something else, indeed," Meg muttered.

"What's that?" Charlie asked, obviously seeking clarification more so than repetition.

"Nothing," Meg replied, forcing a smile. "I should think there are better things to talk about at dinner than my mother."

"Indeed," he agreed. "How are Ruth and Baby Lizzy today? I so missed seeing them, but I had rather a lot of business matters to attend to and getting a Marconi out aboard this vessel is virtually impossible."

"They're well," she replied, smiling. "Ruth asked about you several times today. She was happy to see Mr. Jonaffin, but she wanted to know where you were as well."

He smiled. "That girl is a spitfire if I've met one. I should like to see her running around the factory floor, ordering the workers about, someday soon."

Meg nodded. "That might be a good job for her, though you'd have to be careful she didn't end up in the machinery."

"Yes, of course," he nodded. "You never know where our little Ruth might end up."

She couldn't help but notice he had already taken claim to her, saying "our" little Ruth, which made her a bit melancholy. She hoped that, regardless of what transpired between them, he would keep his promise to Daniel. She was certain he would.

As the fourth course was taken up, she made eye contact with Molly, who winked at her, an assurance that all was still safe. Nevertheless, over an hour into dinner, with at least another five courses to go, Meg could feel the panic growing inside of her. She needed to find a way to get out of the dining room before the inevitable happened and someone recognized her. "Charlie," she said quietly once there was a break in his conversation with the other dinner guests seated around him, "do you think we must stay for the entire dinner?"

Charlie's forehead creased in a look of concern. "Are you feeling all right?"

"Yes," she replied. "I'm just... nervous, that's all."

"You're lookin' a little pale there, Meg," Molly chimed in from across the table. "You need to go lay down?"

Meg couldn't tell if the comment was accurate or if she was just trying to be helpful. She took a sip of water, not sure how to respond.

Charlie spoke up. "If you're not feeling well, we can go. But you have nothing to be nervous about."

"Everyone is staring at me," she reminded him.

Leaning in to her ear, he whispered, "That's because you're beautiful."

Feeling her face redden, she smiled and then replied, "No, it's because they are wondering who I am and what I am doing with you."

"Let them wonder. It's none of their business," he stated dismissively.

Before she could reply, a woman's voice from the other end of the table caught her attention. "Meg, where are you from? Your accent sounds familiar. Southampton?"

It was the woman who had identified herself as Mrs. Appleton. She felt Charlie tense next to her, which she thought was a bit odd, but she proceeded to answer the question the best she could without giving any contradictory information. "Yes, madam," she replied.

"Whereabouts? Eastleigh? Chilworth?"

"Nursling, actually," Meg answered, which was a lie. She had lived in Chilworth her whole life. This woman was good.

"Oh, I have a friend who lives in Nursling. Perhaps you've heard of her. Mrs. Sarah Everton?"

"No, I'm afraid I don't know her," Meg stated, this time the truth.

"Meg, is that short for Margaret then?" the older woman pressed on.

"Well, it ain't short for mega millionaire, I'll tell you that," Molly joked. "Why all the questions, Mrs. Appleton? Can't you see the girl's nervous?"

"There's nothing to be nervous about. I was just trying to be polite," Mrs. Appleton responded, an air of offense in her voice. "I just thought it might be a little ironic for Mr. Ashton to have met another Margaret so quickly, after his last engagement was broken off, that's all."

Before even Molly could prepare a comeback, Meg found herself saying, "Her name is **Mary** Margaret, I believe, not Margaret, and Mrs. Appleton, I'm afraid you've either been listening too intently to the rumor mills or are privy to some sort of insider information; I'm sorry to tell you that you may not know precisely what you are talking about."

"Pardon?" the older woman asked, clearly appalled that a woman of lesser stature would address her in such a way.

"Meg, it's okay," Charlie was saying, his hand on her leg beneath the table.

"No, it's not," she replied in a sharp whisper. "She can't say things like that and think it's all right."

"We warned ya yesterday, Mrs. Appleton, not to be believin' everything you hear out of them rumor mongers," Molly exclaimed, shaking her head.

"Are you saying then, Mrs. Brown, that all of this gossip is false and that Miss Westmoreland didn't elope with the servant boy?"

"What she's saying is that it's none of your business," Meg shot back, pulling her napkin off of her lap and setting it on the table. "Now, if the rest of you fine people will excuse me, I am in need of some fresh air." And with that, despite not wanting to cause a scene, Meg got up from the table as quietly as she could and headed for the nearest exit, keeping her head down and a gloved hand next to her face.

She knew Charlie was probably right behind her, and when she heard footsteps, she assumed they were his. But when she heard her name being called it was in a woman's voice, a voice she recognized. She froze, praying that when she turned around it would be only Madeline standing there.

It wasn't.

"Meg!" Madeline Astor was saying, clearly having followed her across the room. Charlie was standing right behind her, easily within earshot. Meg was only steps away from the door. She had almost made it. "What are you doing here? We'd heard you were in Southampton—some ridiculous rumor about... well, it doesn't matter. You are here after all."

She watched as Charlie's handsome face changed from confusion, to bewilderment, and then to utter outrage, all in the matter of seconds. By the time Madeline turned to address him, he was just managing to mask his emotions enough to fool her. "You must be so happy to be able to bring her out and about at last," she continued, placing her hand lightly on his arm. "Were you ill?" she asked, turning back to Meg.

She nodded. "Yes, and in fact, I was just on my way to get some fresh air, if you'll excuse me."

"Yes, of course," Madeline nodded. "I do hope you feel better soon."

Meg didn't acknowledge her last statement, breaking through the door and making her way as quickly as possible in borrowed shoes to the nearest railing. She leaned over, quite certain she was about to be sick, but the cold air was enough to soothe her flushed skin, and as she cooled off, she began to feel a bit better physically. She wasn't sure she would ever recover emotionally.

She had hoped Charlie might follow her, give her a chance to explain, but she also knew standing outside the First Class Dining Hall was probably not the appropriate place to have a heated conversation. After a few moments, she decided to go back to where she belonged and headed down the closest stairwell on her way back to Steerage.

Charlie had followed Meg out into the hall but had gone no further. Madeline was looking at him expectantly, so of course he had to follow. A million thoughts were running through his mind, so many puzzle pieces suddenly clicking together, and yet there were so many unanswered questions as well. How could this have happened? How could he have been dating his own fiancée without even realizing it? As he stood in the hall attempting to recompose himself, Molly caught up to him. The expression on her face let him know she had more information than he did. "You knew?" he asked.

She nodded. "She told me this afternoon. That's why we were late."

He leaned back against the wall, rubbing his forehead, one arm across his chest supporting his elbow. "Why didn't you tell me?"

"When? On the stairwell?" she scoffed. "Listen, Charlie, you have every right to be angry. But this isn't what you think. Not exactly. You need to talk to her. No, you need to listen to her."

He shook his head. "I can't. Not now. I don't think you realize what she did to me, Molly. I have never been so angry—at anyone—in my entire life."

"I understand that, darlin'. I really do," Molly assured him. There were other people passing through the hallway now, and bearing in mind their primary objective had been to make sure Charlie was able to save face in front of his counterparts, she quietly said, "If you can't talk to her right now, then let's go back to your room, out of the public eye, and we'll get this sorted out."

Charlie highly doubted that was possible, but he also knew standing in the hall outside the dining salon was not the place to be. "Fine," he muttered. She linked her arm through his and he silently escorted her back to his quarters, replaying every conversation he had ever had with Meg over and over in his mind as he went.

CHAPTER 13

As soon as he entered his room, Charlie took off his jacket and tie, tossing them on the back of the sofa before collapsing into his usual chair, his head in his hands. Despite having spent most of the last week feeling like a fool, nothing could possibly top this level of idiocy.

Molly was perched on the arm of the sofa nearby, giving him a moment to collect himself, no doubt. When he didn't speak, she finally said, "Listen, Charlie, there's a lot more to this story than you realize."

"I hope so," he finally muttered. "Otherwise, I am simply the biggest imbecile ever to walk the face of the earth."

"Oh, come on now," she scolded, "that's not true. Charlie, when you hear her side of the story, I think you'll realize this has a lot less to do with you than you think it does."

"Less to do with me?" he asked, sitting up straight. "Molly, we were engaged for three years. Time after time, my parents sent for her so that we could get married at last, and there was always some excuse. Finally, I sail across the ocean to collect my bride, and she's not there. She's nowhere to be found. Are you telling me the rumors about the servant boy aren't true? That she really was kidnapped? Because she seems to be strolling around the promenades pretty independently."

Molly gave him a moment to calm down before she attempted to answer his questions. "What I meant was there are parts of the story you have no knowledge of, darlin', and if you listen to her, if you let her tell you why she made the decisions she did, I think you'll realize your anger is misplaced. Yes, Meg made some bad choices—that's for certain—but there were some pretty good reasons that led her to those choices."

"Well, I'm not going to.... I can't..."

"Take a deep breath and simmer down now, honey."

He took her advice, trying to call himself the best he could, but he was having a very difficult time controlling his emotions. His hands were shaking and he began to feel tears stinging the corner of his eyes.

Molly stood and poured him a brandy, handing it to him before pouring one for herself. He downed it, and she refilled his glass before sitting back down on the arm of the chair. After a few moments, he finally said, "I don't understand why she didn't just tell me."

"She said she tried to," Molly replied.

Charlie considered the statement. Meg had been trying to tell him something last night, something he refused to hear. She'd made him promise not to be angry at Daniel and Kelly once he found out—which told him she knew how he would react. "But why didn't she tell me before? For example, when I first met her?"

"I don't know," Molly admitted. "Maybe she was afraid you'd tell her mother where she's at. Maybe she didn't see the point. She probably didn't think you'd keep running into each other, what with her in Steerage and you up here in First Class. Maybe the real question you need to be asking is, why were you so insistent in pursuing her, even when she told you she had a secret that would push you away?"

"Well, that's simple," he replied. "She's... incredible."

"Do you mean she's beautiful—or do you mean she's an incredible person?"

That question took a bit more thought, but not much. "I mean, of course she's stunning. But the Meg that I met, the one I've spent the last few days with, she's one of the most interesting, well-spoken, intelligent people I've ever known."

Molly nodded. "And what if that Meg—the one you've gotten to know—is the real Meg. And the one that left you in Southampton is the façade?"

Charlie's brain hurt. He ran his hand through his hair and took another sip of brandy. "I don't know, Molly. It's just... I don't understand how she can be the same person. The Meg I knew isn't capable of treating someone with that level of disregard."

"Well, once you hear the full story, I think you'll understand. I think you should go talk to her—tonight. But if not tonight then tomorrow. I know you'll feel better when you do. Now, I am going to go rejoin the ladies, see what they have to say, see what rumors I can quell, that sort of thing."

Charlie stood to escort her to the door. Before he opened it, he wrapped his arms around her and she patted him on the back the way she would her own son in a similar situation. "Thank you for all of your help, Molly," he said quietly.

"Oh, sweetie, I hope I didn't do anything to make it worse. You're a good kid, Charlie. I want you to be happy. You deserve to be happy. And I think Meg's the one for you. But if not, life goes on, my boy. It really does."

He nodded and kissed her on the cheek before opening the door for her and bidding her goodnight. Once she was gone, he retrieved his glass, poured another brandy, and fell back into his chair, wondering absently where Jonathan was, and going over everything in his mind again. The whole thing seemed so surreal. He had attempted to get over a broken heart caused by a runaway bride, with that very same woman—without even knowing it. How could he feel anything except for foolish?

⁂

THE C DECK promenade was fairly busy with families and couples out and about enjoying the evening after dinner, preparing to return to their cabins in just a bit, or perhaps to another party similar to the one the night before. While she couldn't say she didn't catch a few stares, dressed as she was, for the most part, she was able to keep to herself and wound her way over to a less busy part of the boat.

She ended up leaning against the railing not too far from the bench she had shared with Charlie the night prior. Perhaps, subconsciously, she had thought he might know to look for her there, should he choose to give her the opportunity to explain. Or perhaps she simply knew the view here was spectacular. Either way, she was alone now, staring out at the dark blue abyss below her, hoping that Molly was able to handle whatever damage she had left in her wake.

It wasn't as if she hadn't had plenty of time to prepare herself for this. She'd known all along that he would react precisely the way he had, though she was actually surprised he had let her go without chasing her down and yelling at her. Maybe that would still happen, though she doubted it. He was an extremely level-headed person, and while she still expected to face him, she was fairly certain he was more likely to be disappointed than angry. In a way, she had actually wished he would have followed her, called her every name in the book. At least then she'd know how he was doing. Now, she could only assume he was somewhere cursing her name. Or perhaps she had meant so little to him that he was able to shrug it off and go on about his way.

She didn't think that was the case, however. No, she was quite confident that Charlie was brokenhearted again—at her hand. The feelings of despair and guilt she was wallowing in now were well deserved, and within a few minutes she found herself struggling to hold back her tears. But she refused to let herself break down. She didn't deserve it. How could she cry over someone she had willingly given up? Any personal pain she felt at the loss of a relationship with Charles Ashton was self-induced, and therefore, should garner no sympathy from anyone, including herself.

Familiar footsteps behind her caught her attention sooner than she had expected; she thought it would take at least a few hours before Jonathan hunted her down. As he came to rest on the railing beside her, she couldn't muster enough courage to look at him, and they stood there in silence for a long moment, staring at the ocean.

Eventually, he asked, "How is he?"

Puzzled, she turned and looked at him then. "You don't know?" she asked. He shook his head, and she returned her focus to the more welcoming frigid Atlantic before she said, "I'm not sure. Angry, I would guess. Disappointed. Stunned, perhaps."

Jonathan was silent again for quite some time before he asked, "Was there a scene?"

"No," she assured him. "Well, not over that. I may have pissed off Mrs. Appleton before I left." He actually snickered at that, which she found strange considering the circumstances. Then she added, "I think he's probably with Molly."

"Good," Jonathan replied. "He shouldn't be alone."

She agreed. "I just assumed he'd sent you. Or he'd told you what happened, and you came to... give me what for."

"No, I haven't seen him since before dinner. I had plans myself but ended up cutting them just a bit short so that I could come and find you," he explained.

"With who?" she asked quietly.

"Christine," he replied. She nodded in acknowledgement, and he said no more, knowing he didn't have to.

"So then you know... everything," she stated, returning her gaze out to the sea.

"Yes."

"Who else...?"

"I made her promise not to say anything to anyone, or else I would let Mrs. Brown know she'd been eavesdropping, and she'd lose her employment. Of course, the only reason she was eavesdropping in the first place was because I paid her to do so, but that is neither here nor there."

Meg shook her head. "I knew you were good at your job, but I didn't see that coming."

"What can I say? You're right. I've got to know what's imminent before it happens. I've already fallen short of protecting him—twice— in the same week—from the same girl. I was desperate to find out who you are and what you wanted. Now that I know, well, we just need to find a way to fix this."

Meg looked at him in shock. "Fix it?" she asked. She was having a hard time believing what she was hearing. "What do you mean?"

"I mean... you make Charlie happy. And even though he's probably cursing your name right now—both of them—once he hears the whole story, I think he'll understand more than you give him credit for," Jonathan explained.

Though she wanted to believe what he was saying was possible, that there might be a chance she could reconcile with Charlie, she just couldn't bear to get her hopes up, only to have them come crashing down again. "But what I did to him was... horrible."

"Oh, I know. You don't have to tell me. I was there, remember?"

Meg nodded, dropping her eyes back to the water.

"But when he hears everything you've been through, for so long, he'll understand. And he'll be outraged at your mother and uncle, too, that's for certain. You can be sure he'll do whatever he can to make sure they pay for what they've done to you."

Meg couldn't bear to think about that presently, so she pushed those despicable thoughts aside. "But what about Ezra?" she asked. "Surely, he'll be angry about that."

"Possibly," he admitted. "I'm really not sure. I mean, desperate times call for desperate measures. It's not as if Charlie is a saint himself you know. There was a time, before he was officially engaged to you, that he was a bit of a playboy."

She didn't know, though she had assumed he'd probably been with a woman or two. Still, standards were different for men, and she could easily see some men being very unforgiving when it came to a woman's virtue—especially when she had the audacity to sleep with another man when she was supposed to be meeting her fiancé for the first time. Nevertheless, she saw no reason to go into such a discussion with Jonathan now.

She began to realize there was a very small possibility that she actually might end up with Charlie after all, but the fear of accepting that prospect was almost overwhelming. Those tears she had been fighting back for over an hour now were threatening to spill over. She clenched her eyes tightly and took a few deep breaths, putting all of her energy toward regaining her composure. Finally, she turned to him, looked him in the eyes and said, "Jonathan, will you help me?"

"Of course," he said, and she flung herself into his arms, no longer able to contain her emotions. "It's all right, Meg. Don't cry. Everything will be all right."

But she realized that he was crying as well, and after a few moments, she pulled away a bit so that she could look at him. "Jonathan, why would you..." she began swiping at the tears streaming down her face. "I don't understand...."

He managed a small smile, and using his thumb, he gently wiped a tear from her cheek. "I just want him to be happy. You can do that, Meg, can't you?"

"Yes," she nodded. "I know I can. If he'll just give me one more chance."

He nodded in return and pulled her back into his arms. "It will take time. This isn't something we can fix overnight. But if we work together, I think we can make him see why you did the things you did. In the meantime, you just need to stay in Steerage, make yourself invisible, and wait for him to come to you, all right?"

"All right," she nodded. "I can do that."

"Good. Now, let me go see what I can do."

CHAPTER 14

"What do you mean you think I should go talk to her? Are you mad? You of all people should know everything I've been through. The last thing I need to do is go talk to her!"

"Well, no, not right now," Jonathan admitted. He had only been in Charlie's stateroom for a few minutes, but he had easily ascertained that his friend was hammered, a rarity. "Right now, what you need to do is put that bottle of Jameson down and go sleep this one off."

"You don't understand, Jonathan. She. Lied. To. Me. Again!" He was standing on the outside deck, bottle in one hand, glass in the other, his shirt mostly unbuttoned, shoes off, still in his suit pants, and Jonathan was doing his best to ensure he kept his voice low enough that the other First Class passengers nearby in their staterooms couldn't hear him.

"Why don't you come inside, and we'll talk about it in there?" he asked for about the tenth time since his arrival.

"Nope. Huh uh. I paid for this deck, and goddammit, I'm gonna use it," he replied dropping into a chair and taking a swig directly out of the whiskey bottle.

"Fine, then I'll sit right next to you so that you don't have to yell. How's that?" Jonathan asked, taking a seat.

"Fine. But I don't want to talk about it. Not now. I'm done talking about it."

"That's fine. We don't have to..."

"To hell with her, whatever the... hell her name is... Mary Margaret Meg Westmoreland—West whore land..."

"Charlie..."

"Don't defend her. You always defend her!" Charlie said, pointing a finger at him, despite the fact that he was still holding the empty glass in the same hand.

"I'm not," Jonathan assured him. "I'm not defending her. I'm just saying you don't want the other passengers to hear you calling her names, that's all."

"What other passengers?" Charlie said rather loudly. "Look around! We're alone!"

"There are other passengers in the cabins next to us, above us, and below us, Charlie. Come on, you know that. And we need to make sure none of them have any suspicions that the rumors they are hearing are true. So, again, why don't we come inside, get some sleep, and we'll talk about it in the morning, all right?"

"What about the deck?"

"The deck will still be here in the morning. We'll be in this ship for at least another four days. So, come on now," he said, pulling Charlie up by the arms. This time, Charlie was actually compliant, surprisingly, and he was able to get him within a few steps of the door before he pulled away and approached the railing. Sighing, Jonathan asked, "What are you doing now?"

"This glass will not be making the journey to New York City," he explained before pitching it off the side of the *Titanic* far out into open sea.

"You are so odd when you're drunk," Jonathan muttered. "Fair enough. Now come on before you fall overboard yourself. I'm sure that water is quite cold. Let's not find out."

MEG HAD HARDLY SLEPT at all the night of April 13. She began to drift off a few times, but each time she did so, memories of what had transpired between herself and Charlie came flooding back to her. She replayed conversations in her mind, memories of his touch, his kisses, and then that myriad of expressions on his face when he realized her betrayal for the second time. She had no way of knowing what had transpired between Jonathan and Charlie last night, if Molly was able to delay the rumor mills, or if she had ended up ruining his reputation once and for all. And the only way she would find out is if someone came to tell her. She planned to follow Jonathan's advice to a T, vowing not to even leave her cabin unless it was to speak to Charlie.

So, when the rest of the family went out for breakfast, she stayed behind. She had carefully folded the dress she had borrowed from Lady Lucy Duff Gordon, the shoes, jewelry, and all of the other pieces, and stowed them beneath her bed wrapped in an extra blanket so that Ruth or Lizzy wouldn't want to touch them. Dressed in a Third Class skirt and shirtwaist she had borrowed from Kelly before they left Southampton, she began to wonder exactly who she was again. Switching from First Class to Third and back again was taxing, as was the pressure of knowing some of the ships passengers knew her true identity while others did not. Perhaps it was best that she would not be interacting with many people. Who knows what she might end up saying?

She had only a few moments to talk to Kelly that morning before she left with Daniel and the girls for breakfast. She had asked how it went, and Meg simply shook her head. "He found out then?" Kelly clarified.

"Yes."

"How?"

"Madeline."

"I see. And?"

"I left. I haven't spoken to him. I'm sure he doesn't want to speak to me at all, but should he change his mind, he knows where to find me."

"I'm so sorry, Meg," she had said, giving her friend a quick hug before leaving with a promise of bringing her some toast and fruit when they returned.

In the meantime, Meg was left with very little to do except to try to read her book and push thoughts of Charles Ashton out of her head.

⚬❧⚬

IT WAS past noon when Charlie finally awoke, and he wasn't sure which was more painful, the pounding in his head or the ache in his heart. One reminded him of the other, and for a very brief moment, he contemplated a quick splash over the side of the deck to put himself out of this misery. He knew that wasn't really an option, however, and when he finally managed to open one eye, he was relieved to see that Jonathan had at least set some aspirin and water on his nightstand. It wouldn't do much for his head, and nothing at all for his heart, but it was a start.

After downing the pills and hiding his head under the pillow for a few more moments, he finally managed to pull himself out of bed and stumble to the bathroom. His room was only one of four on the entire ship with a private bathroom, and today he was very thankful he had paid the extra money to have such facilities nearby. It wouldn't do for the rest of the First Class passengers to see how completely hung-over he was.

He heard a stirring from the main living quarters and emerged from the bathroom to find Jonathan with an array of potential brunch items. "Good morning," he said. "I'm guessing you're probably not hungry, but I did order some dry toast—which I think is probably your best option. And possibly some orange juice."

Charlie waved both items away and dropped onto the couch on his back. "Why is the sun so bright?" he asked, tossing a pillow over his face.

"Let me turn it down for you," Jonathan said sarcastically. He did, however, adjust the blinds to make sure they were closed as tightly as possible.

"How much did I drink?" Charlie asked, pressing the pillow against his eyes.

"From what I can tell, about a bottle of brandy, and most of a bottle of Jameson."

"Don't ever let me drink alcohol again, all right?" he said, muffled by the pillow.

Jonathan didn't bother to acknowledge that statement. "Listen, I know you feel like shit, but it's past noon, and I really think you should consider going down to talk to Meg."

Charlie pulled the pillow back to look at him. "What?" he asked, not sure he had heard correctly. "Whatever are you talking about? You know who she is, don't you?"

Realizing he must not remember any bits of the conversation they had, had the night before, Jonathan replied, "Yes, I know who she is. And I also know why she lied to you. I know you're hurt and angry—rightfully so—but I think you'll feel better once you let her explain."

"No," Charlie said, placing the pillow back over his face.

"Charlie," Jonathan coaxed, "just give her a chance to tell you what happened. Otherwise, you'll always regret not knowing the whole truth."

"The truth is she chose not to be with me, thought she'd rather spend her time with some servant boy, and then lied to me about who she was. Why in the world would I ever want to see her again?" He had somehow managed to sit up and face Jonathan, who was sitting in the chair across from him now, though Charlie wasn't quite sure where this new found physical strength was coming from, his inner rage, perhaps.

Shaking his head, Jonathan said, "You don't understand...."

"I don't understand? No, Jonathan, you don't understand. How can you possibly take her side? You of all people who have watched me suffer over this for a week—longer than that, really, when you factor in all of my wallowing over why she never wrote a letter or sent a photo."

Jonathan realized they were rehashing the exact same conversation they had, had the night before, though there was a distinct possibility that Charlie had no memory of it whatsoever. He repeated himself, however, simply because there was no other choice but to do so. "Charlie, I'm not taking her side. I'm taking your side. I'm always on your side. Listen, I know why Meg made the choices she made now. You need to talk to her yourself so she can explain it to you in person."

"How do you know?" he asked, a confused expression on his face.

"It doesn't matter," Jonathan replied, preferring not to explain the entire situation again. "Just do it. You'll feel much better about yourself when you do."

Charlie absorbed what he was saying, but the thought of seeing Meg again, of sitting across from her and letting her elucidate some rationale for her behavior, was somewhat terrifying. As much as he would like to believe Jonathan—and Molly—when they said speaking to her would ease his conscience, he didn't know how that was possible. He did believe, however, that seeing her again could easily make him remember just how much he wanted to be with her, which could potentially start this entire vicious cycle all over again, something he was not willing to subject himself to. "Listen, Jonathan, I appreciate the fact that you want me to have some closure, but not today. I can't deal with that today."

"I don't want you to have closure. I want you to have Meg. And if you go and talk to her, I think you will."

Charlie eyed him skeptically. "I don't know how that's possible. I can't believe there's anything she could possibly say that would make me forgive what she's done."

"I disagree."

"How is that possible?"

"Go talk to her, and you'll see," Jonathan urged. "You can wait until tomorrow, or the next day, or next week, but ultimately, you're just torturing yourself. Go, hear her out. Or I'll bring her here. Whichever you prefer. You just need to hear what she has to say."

Running his hands through his short brown hair, once again, Charlie considered what his friend was saying. Perhaps he was right. Maybe not. Either way, he was in no mental state to talk to anyone just now. "I'll think about it," he finally said. "But right now, I'm going to go utilize that bath tub I paid thousands of dollars for."

As Charlie left the room, Jonathan shook his head, unsure precisely what he should do. He had spoken to Molly earlier that day, and she had filled him in on the state of the now very confused First Class socialites. Some people insisted that it was not Mary Margaret who had accompanied Charlie to dinner the night before—that he had simply invited a girl from Third Class, one he had rescued from falling overboard, perhaps. Others, such as Madeline Astor herself, insisted that she had spoken to Mary Margaret and knew for a fact it was her. Then there was the idea that the girl was Mary Margaret pretending to be someone else. The entire rumor mill was confused, and new speculations and inaccuracies were floating about by the moment. If Charlie were to truly patch things over with Meg, it would make it much easier to shut everyone up completely. And while that didn't necessarily have to be done immediately, the sooner it happened the better.

It wasn't often that Jonathan made decisions that went against Charlie's wishes, but in this particular instance, he knew what he needed to do, and as far as he was concerned, time was truly of the essence.

CHAPTER 15

eg had just dozed off when a knocking on the cabin door jarred her awake. The family had come back briefly after breakfast, delivering the promised food stuffs, and then set out again. This time, Ruth was determined to see an "ocapus," and even though her parents warned her that Uncle Charlie probably wouldn't be around to help her find one, she was hopeful he would show up.

She wasn't the only one.

But Meg was fairly certain when she reached the door, it wouldn't be him on the other side. Pulling it open to find Jonathan standing in the hall, therefore, was not disappointing.

"I think you should come with me," he said, not even bothering with a greeting.

Meg ran a hand through her disheveled hair. "Does he want to see me?" she asked, confused.

"Not necessarily," Jonathan admitted. "But I think you should still come with me."

"To Charlie's stateroom?"

"Yes."

"Uninvited?"

"Invited by me."

She considered the proposition again. "But what if he...."

"Meg, what could possibly be worse?"

He had a point. "All right. Can I bring the dress and other items I need to return to Molly?"

"Of course," he replied and waited for her to go and fetch them from beneath the bed.

She kept them wrapped in the blanket so they wouldn't be so awkward to carry, and they made their way up and over to First Class.

Jonathan was unusually quiet as they walked along, and Meg was hesitant to speak. At one point, she did ask, "Is Charlie's room near Mrs. Brown's?" and was answered with a quiet, "No." She was left wondering what she might be doing with the dress and other items then, which he had insisted on carrying for her, but she soon realized she was only so focused on returning those items because she didn't want to think about the conversation she was about to have with Charlie—if he would even speak to her at all.

Upon reaching the stateroom, Jonathan ushered her into the parlor. They could hear Charlie in the bedroom, and the valet clearly wanted to make sure he spoke to Charlie before he discovered Meg's presence. "Have a seat," Jonathan said, and rushed off into the adjoining room.

She had traveled on luxurious ocean liners before, but she had never seen anything quite like this stateroom. The furniture was Georgian, whereas Mrs. Brown's had been Louis XV, and the sheer size of the space was also quite impressive. As she sat in the chair Jonathan had pointed out for what seemed an eternity, she could hear their muffled exchange coming from the other room, and though she could not understand what was being said, it was clear Charlie was not happy that Jonathan had retrieved her without his permission. She began to glance nervously at the door, pondering the possibility of just walking out. As time went by, the idea seemed more and more appealing, and she had just placed her hand on the armchair to push herself up to standing when the bedroom door opened.

Charlie looked terrible--for Charlie anyway, which compared to most people still made him quite handsome, but she couldn't help but notice that he looked ill. His skin was pale, his hair was damp, there were bags beneath his eyes, which were bloodshot, and even though he was neatly dressed, she couldn't help but think he had just thrown on his clothes because she was there.

He stood behind the sofa, across the room from her, just staring. Even when Jonathan exited the bedroom, clearly on his way to deliver the outfit to Mrs. Brown, he did not take his eyes off of her. Finally, she stood, saying, "I shouldn't stay."

"You shouldn't have come."

She nodded once, sharply.

"But you're here, so you might as well stay."

Meg hesitated, not sure if he really meant it or not. She glanced at the door, and then back at him. He hadn't moved. Her eyes darted to the door again.

"Sit down, Mary Margaret."

She complied.

Charlie continued to stand behind the sofa, his hands pushed deep into his pants pockets for a few more seconds before he finally walked around the corner and sat down on the edge of the cushion, his elbows on his knees, leaning forward, staring at her. She was extremely uncomfortable, but she deserved every second of it. When he didn't speak, she cleared her throat nervously. He still said nothing. When she could stand it no more, she asked quietly, "Are you well?"

He scoffed, shaking his head, just a touch, slowly from side to side, finally looking away from her. Still, he said nothing.

"What I meant to say, is are you ill?"

"I know what you meant to say," he assured her. "I'm not ill. I'm very hung-over."

"I'm sorry," she said quietly, shifting her position slightly in the chair.

"You should be."

"I meant... about the... I mean, of course I'm sorry...."

"I know what you meant, Mary Margaret."

"I'm still Meg."

"Not to me you're not."

The sting of those words hit hard, and she instantly felt the tears hit the corners of her eyes. She noticed a flicker of a smile then, as if he was happy to have gotten that reaction, but she knew she deserved anything he sent her way, so she endured it.

He scooted back on the couch then, resting one ankle on the opposite knee, his elbow on the arm rest, his head on his fist. "What is this vitally important piece of information that you're about to share with me that will make me realize I should forgive you? That all of this is really all my fault?"

"It's not your fault, not at all. If someone said something to make you think that I have ever implied that you've done anything to deserve the way I've treated you then they are sadly mistaken," she interjected quickly. If he heard nothing else she said, ever again for the rest of her life, then he at least had to hear—and understand—that.

"Then what is it, Mary Margaret? What is it that you've come to tell me?"

Even at this distance the piercing nature of his green eyes locked on her in such a way made it very challenging for her to think, and even under normal circumstances it was extremely difficult for her to tell the story of what had brought her to this point. She wasn't quite sure what to say or where to start. She certainly didn't want to rehash exactly what she had conveyed to Molly. Rather than starting at the beginning, she decided to start at the end. "The reason I told you I wasn't good enough for you, the other night, after the dance, was because it's true. I haven't been good enough for you for quite some time. And over the years, that knowledge has caused me to make some terrible decisions, many of which, I'm afraid, were made without even taking you into consideration, for which I'm truly sorry, but I would be lying if I didn't say that I don't think I ever really saw you as a person until I glimpsed you outside of my home just a few mornings ago. All of those years, I guess I just assumed you were as upset about the arrangement as I was, and that if I could find a way to end it, we'd both be happy." She paused then, waiting to see if he had anything to say. She could tell he was considering her words, so she gave him time to process.

After several moments, she decided to press on; however, just as she was about to continue, he asked, "When you say you were not good enough for me, what do you mean by that?"

She sighed, closed her eyes tightly, and then opened them again, avoiding his stare. "I meant, I was... ruined."

His expression did not change. "And when you say for quite some time, for how long are you referring?"

She shook her head, not quite sure, not wanting to think back that far. Finally, she said, "Thirteen years, I suppose."

There was a reaction then as his eyes widened. "Thirteen years? But you're only twenty."

"Yes."

"But how...." She watched as his expression changed from pure puzzlement to extreme outrage. "My God. Your uncle?"

"Yes."

"You should have told me."

"How? Everything I sent to you was censored. Nothing left our home without close scrutiny."

"There must have been someone you could tell. Your mother?"

"Ha!" She rolled her eyes.

"A neighbor or a family friend perhaps?"

"Charlie, everyone I told ended up injured or bribed. No one would listen to me. Besides... for the longest time... I was convinced it was my own fault."

"Surely you don't believe that now?"

She could no longer meet his gaze, choosing instead to look down at the borrowed dress she wore, her hands fidgeting with a frayed hem.

"Meg, you know that's not your fault now, don't you?"

The fact that he had used her nickname again was not lost on her, but it still took her a moment to answer. At last she said, "It doesn't matter. There was another choice, one that was my own, which had the same result."

"The servant boy?"

"Ezra."

"On the night of the ball?"

"I planned to run away with him. But, in my mind, I wasn't running from you. I was running from them."

He was shaking his head again.

"When he decided to leave with another woman, I realized I still had to go. I certainly couldn't try to patch things over with you, not after the way I had disrespected you. And I knew my mother and uncle simply wanted your money anyway. I decided to escape to America, to become someone else, to leave my family behind. In my mind, I suppose, I thought you'd be happy. You'd be free."

"Were you home the day I came to call at your house the first time?"

"Yes."

"Were you truly ill?"

"No."

He raised his eyebrows, awaiting an explanation.

"I was... injured."

He exhaled loudly, shaking his head again, looking away. "I wish you would have trusted me to say something then, to signal me or get my attention somehow. I would have helped you."

"I know," she assured him. "I know that. But I overheard what you said to my mother, about how you had no idea where to even begin in finding a new wife. She assured you that you wouldn't have to, that my setback was temporary. I was so angry that she was bartering with me. In my mind, all I ever was, was a way for my mother to rebuild her fortune. I never stopped to consider my father's thinking when he picked you for me. Not until it was too late."

"When was it too late?"

She considered his question for a moment, thinking truly only he could answer that. But she was certain he meant when was it too late by her consideration. "If I'm honest, it's been too late since the first time the boogeyman snuck into my room. But what I meant to say was, had I considered the care and devotion my father put into planning this arrangement with your father before he died, if I had been thinking in those terms all along, I would have realized that my engagement to you was a gift, not a burden."

"So you boarded the *Titanic* planning to sail to America, to find a job, and somehow blend in amongst the common class?"

"Yes."

"And Ruth chose me to run to out of all of those people all by herself?"

"Most certainly. I truly had no idea where she had gone. Surely, you don't doubt that?"

He was silent for a long moment, his eyes focused on the floor. "I was actually looking for you anyway."

"What?"

"I'd seen you at the launch, noticed how beautiful you were, thought you could take my mind off of my estranged fiancée. How ironic is that?"

She chose to ignore his pointed question. "So, you were on the Third Class promenade looking for me?"

"Yes."

"Well, I'm glad you found me. Look, Charlie, I did intend to contact you once I reached the States, one way or another, to let you know none of this was your fault. But I had to be absolutely certain my mother and uncle could never find me. I know everything that has happened aboard the *Titanic* has complicated things to no end, but I'm not sorry any of this has happened. I have a lot of regrets, many of which I've hashed out for you today. But the time I spent with you here certainly is not one of them. If nothing else, it made me realize how foolish I've been for so long. Not only have I never met a man like you, I would have never dreamt anyone like you even existed." He scoffed, shaking his head again. "Don't do that. I'm serious." She pushed herself to the edge of the seat, but she didn't dare approach him. "You are absolutely perfect in every way, and the fact that you're doubting that because of me... that's the worst punishment I could possibly receive, perhaps even worse than a sentence of life without you."

He locked eyes with her then, and for once she was not tempted to look away for quite some time. Eventually, he dropped his gaze back to the interesting spot in the carpet, and she said, "I should go. I've taken up enough of your time." The irony in the phrase was not intended, but it was recognized by them both, she was sure.

She stood and approached the door, certain she would locate Jonathan nearby, and he would walk her back to E Deck if she wanted him to. Just as she was about to reach for the knob, she felt his hand on her shoulder, and she turned and buried her face in his neck, no longer able to hold back her tears. He wrapped his arms tightly around her, smoothing her hair, letting her cry. After several moments, she finally began to pull herself together, and she stepped back brushing at the remnants on her cheeks with her fingertips.

She could tell by his expression that he still didn't quite trust her, and she didn't blame him, but he wouldn't be standing there if he didn't care about her. And that, if nothing more, was hope.

"It'll be all right, Meg," he promised.

She nodded. "I should go."

"Jonathan will walk you back."

She nodded again, and he opened the door for her, softly telling her goodbye.

Jonathan was standing a few feet away. "Are you all right?" he asked as she approached.

"No, but I think I will be. Someday."

"And Charlie?"

"That's completely up to him."

CHAPTER 16

Meg had gone to bed fairly early that night. After returning to the cabin, she'd gone over everything with Kelly, cried some more, and then read for a bit before falling asleep around seven o'clock. Her exhaustion from the night before had caught up to her at last. A few hours later, a strange sensation jarred her from sleep, and even though she had been resting quite some time, she was suddenly wide awake.

She glanced around the darkened room and realized everyone else was still sleeping soundly. The idea of rolling back over and returning to sleep seemed like a good one, but the uneasiness in the pit of her stomach stayed with her, and she decided to go out and investigate.

Taking the extra time to change into clothes, she pulled her shawl around her as well and went out into the hallway. There were a few other passengers out and about, all of them with curious expressions on their faces. "Did you feel something, too?" she asked another woman, still in her nightdress and robe, standing near the end of the hall.

"Yes," she confirmed. "It felt like a vibration of some sort."

"I think I'll go up and investigate," Meg said. She contemplated waking the rest of the family, but she wanted to be sure there was reason to, especially before waking the little girls.

As soon as she reached the upper deck, she could see there was clearly something wrong. There were all sorts of crew members scurrying about, and she could hear them shouting to one another, even from the other decks. Without bothering to stop one of them and ask what was amiss, she headed back down to E Deck to wake up Kelly and Daniel.

By the time Meg returned to the cabin, the floor beneath her feet was damp. She could hear several loud noises, which she assumed were coming from below the passenger compartments in the ship's hull. The light in the cabin was on, and she could hear the family bustling about before she even opened the door.

"Meg!" Kelly exclaimed. "The steward just stopped by. He said we're to put our lifebelts on and head upstairs. What's going on?"

"I'm not sure," she admitted, "but there's a lot of commotion up there. I think it's best if we head straight to the Boat Deck, to the lifeboats. If something's wrong with the ship, we'll want to get you and the girls on a lifeboat straightaway."

"Are we going on the little ship to the other big boat now?" Ruth asked in her sleepy little voice.

"I'm not sure," Kelly admitted. "It'll be fine darlin'. Don't you worry."

Despite his cast, Daniel helped her change into her warmest clothes and was wrapping a shawl around her shoulder as Kelly finished dressing the baby. "I'm going to go back up. Head on over by the stairwell. I'll meet you there in a few minutes," Meg said. Kelly nodded and Meg went back down the hallway, this time with a lifebelt in her hand, which she began to put on as she went.

There were even more people standing about now, though most of them were simply standing in the stairwell or the corridor, not actually attempting to make their way to the Boat Deck. Meg could hear several different languages being spoken around her, and she wondered how many of these people could even read the signs to locate the Boat Deck.

Though she still wasn't quite sure anything was the matter, she instinctively began to formulate a plan. If the crew were actually launching lifeboats when they got there, she would make sure that Kelly and the girls were on one, Daniel, too, if they would let him go. Then, she would try to find Charlie, and make it back to the boats herself. She still wasn't sure he would want to see her at all, but she could hardly get on a lifeboat without first checking to make sure he was all right.

Making her way back the short distance to the stairwell was a bit of a challenge, but she was able to squeeze her way through the curious passengers lining the walkway, and she decided to wait at the landing at the top of the stairs. A moment later, she saw Kelly, carrying Baby Lizzy and Daniel reach the top of the stairs. "Which way do we go?" Kelly asked, peering through the growing crowd.

Meg was puzzled. "Where's Ruth?" she asked, looking around, particularly near their legs.

"She's right here," Kelly said, glancing behind her. "Daniel, don't you have Ruth's hand?"

"I thought she was with you."

Kelly began to panic. "Ruth? RUTH!" All three of them began to scour the crowd, searching everywhere, but Ruth was nowhere to be found. "Oh, my God, what are we going to do?"

"Listen, you need to get up to the Boat Deck," Meg said, attempting to keep her voice calm. "You have to get Lizzy up there, just in case there is a real emergency."

"I'm not leaving here without Ruth," Kelly insisted.

"Kelly, Meg's right," Daniel agreed. "Let us look for Ruth, and you take Lizzy upstairs."

The panic on Kelly's face was increasing by the moment, and Meg was certain there was no way she'd make it to the Boat Deck alone. "Daniel, you're going to have to take her, and make sure she gets on a boat if they're launching. Otherwise, she's not going to go."

"I can't leave here without Ruth," he replied.

"Lizzy needs her mother. I can't take her. It has to be Kelly. I'll find Ruth. She's got to be nearby. We're wasting time. Take Kelly to the Boat Deck, and then come back here. If you don't see me, then that means I haven't found her yet. Start searching, but if you don't find her quickly, we'll need to check in at this stairwell every twenty minutes or so until one of us finds her, all right?"

Daniel could tell she was thinking more clearly than he was. Nodding, he grabbed his wife by the shoulder and began to steer her in the direction of the passages that led to the Boat Deck. "Find my baby, Meg," he yelled over his shoulder as Kelly began to shriek.

Meg pushed her way back down the stairs in pursuit of her niece, yelling her name as she went, and asking anyone whose attention she could get if they had seen a little, red-haired girl. By the time she reached their cabin, she was standing in several inches of water. She threw open the door, hopeful that she would discover the little one. At first glance, the room was empty, but she went to check the beds, just in case. There, in Ruth's bunk, wedged between the mattress and the wall, she found Dolly New Eyes and realized Ruth must have come back in order to retrieve her toy.

Except she didn't make it this far. Which meant she probably took a wrong turn. Grabbing the doll, she went back out the way she had come, the icy water brushing against her ankles now, and headed toward the stairwell. Chances were, if Ruth had made it to the stairs, this was where she had gone wrong. The stairs continued down to F Deck, and if one wasn't paying careful attention, it was easy to miss the landing for E Deck, especially if one were short and in a crowd.

The water was definitely deeper as she made her way further down, though it was not proportionately so. She couldn't quite explain how the water must be entering the boat that there was water on E Deck but F Deck was not completely underwater yet, but she thought it might have something to do with those famous watertight doors. There were not as many people down here, either. Perhaps because they had already made their exit, or maybe there just weren't as many rooms on this deck, either way, what lay before her were mostly darkened, widening passages. And water—more and more water.

ONCE KELLY REALIZED she was slowing their progress by continuing to fight her husband, he was able to get her through the crowd and up the Boat Deck much more quickly. He was quite surprised at how few people were actually present atop the Boat Deck. Though there were quite a few First Class passengers, particularly women, he saw very few Second or Third Class passengers at all.

They were approaching the bow of the ship on the starboard side when Kelly spotted Jonathan and Charlie, who were walking quickly toward them, as if they had already seen the family from afar. "Charlie! Jonathan!" she yelled. "Thank God we found you. Do you know what's going on?"

"Apparently, we've struck an iceberg," Charlie replied. "We were told to make our way up, but it really doesn't seem to be all that serious. Where are Meg and Ruth?"

"Ruth took off again, and Meg went back to find her," Daniel explained.

"Oh, no," Charlie said quietly. "I should go look for them. I'm sure we've nothing to worry about, but just in case."

"Charlie, when we left, there was already water down there," Kelly explained.

"Water? On E Deck?" he clarified, surprise evident in his voice.

"Yes, and now that Kelly and Lizzy are up here with the lifeboats, I'm going back to look for them myself," Daniel stated emphatically.

Charlie nodded as the realization that the information the stewards had given as they woke the passengers just half an hour ago was likely inaccurate began to sink in; this was more than just a precaution. "All right. Jonathan, take Kelly and Lizzy to the bow. That seems to be the place where they are preparing to launch the boats, and Daniel and I will go retrieve Meg and Ruth."

"What? No, I need to come with you," Jonathan replied.

Charlie pulled his valet a few steps to the side, out of earshot. "Listen, Daniel needs to search for his daughter, and Kelly is in no state to stay here alone. When those boats launch, and I believe they will, you need to make sure she gets on. She's a Third Class passenger. They're not likely to put her on first unless you see that they do. And if there's room, you get on, too."

"You can't honestly expect me to get on a lifeboat while you're still on a sinking ship," Jonathan protested.

"I do. If you can, get on. Don't worry about me. I'll be much more likely to find my way out of here if I'm on my own. Which means I've got to find Meg before those boats launch. Now stop arguing and go."

Jonathan inhaled sharply, clearly not approving of his assignment, but he also realized he would not change Charlie's mind, and he was right in his assumption that time was ticking by more quickly than ever now. "Fine," he acquiesced. "But take this." He reached into his coat pocket and produced a small golden key.

"What's this?" Charlie asked eyeing it peculiarly.

"It's a master key to all of the gates below deck. Just in case."

Charlie nodded, not bothering to question how the key had been procured, gave his friend a quick hug, and then took off, Daniel in tow.

"Where did you see them last?" he asked as they made their way through passengers who were attempting to ascend using the same stairways they were using to descend.

"Meg said to meet her at the top of the stairs on E Deck near our cabin if she found Ruth. She said we'd need to check back every twenty minutes or so, so if she found her, that's likely where she'd be."

"If she found Ruth, she'd be up here by now. She would hand her off and then go searching for you. I'm certain we'd run into her on our way back to E Deck if she's there. While that's a good idea, I'm not sure how much time we have. So, you go ahead and go back to F Deck the way you came. I will go down to Scotland Road and search through there. If you find Ruth, get her on a boat. Don't wait."

"How will I know if you find her?"

"I'll find you."

⚜

MEG FELT like she had been searching for Ruth for hours. She had checked so many identical passages, she had no idea of knowing for sure where she had been and where she hadn't. The water had reached her knees, which would be close to Ruth's chest by now, and her voice was hoarse from yelling. She knew she'd told Daniel to meet her every twenty minutes, but at this point, she wasn't even sure which way she needed to go to reach the stairwell on E Deck, and though it had crossed her mind that he might have found his daughter himself by now, she was determined to keep looking until she could no longer move. She'd made a promise to Ruth and her family that she'd never lose her again. She was going to find Ruth or die trying.

The longer she searched, the more she began to think it might just be the latter. She checked every room she came to. Occasionally, she'd run into another passenger, usually one who didn't speak English, and they were often of little help to each other. She desperately wished Charlie was with her. She knew he would know exactly what to do. Ruth would find him, no doubt. But as the minutes wore on, and the water grew deeper, she began to think she would likely never see Charlie again.

She came to another intersection. She looked one way and then the other. The lights began to flicker. She wasn't quite sure which way she had come from. She had been able to keep track by the depth of the water to some degree. If the water was getting higher, she likely hadn't been that way. But the water was beginning to get so deep, she could no longer tell by using this method. She looked to the left, and then to the right, and was just about to choose right when a faint sound to her left caught her attention.

At first, she thought it might have been her imagination. She stood perfectly still, listening to the soft whoosh of the water around her, the humming of the light bulbs, but then she heard it again. It was the sound of a child crying. And it was coming from her left. "Ruth?" she yelled, hurrying in that direction. "Ruth? Is that you? It's Aunt Meg! RUTH!" she came to another intersection and stopped, listening. "RUTH!!!"

Faintly, off in the distance down a dark and flooded corridor, she heard the sweetest sound she'd ever heard. "Aunt Meg?"

"RUTH! Baby bang on something, anything, so I can find you! Don't move! Just bang on the wall!" She had new found strength now and took off running as fast as she could, the icy cold water lapping at her hips no longer a deterrent. She could hear the sound of tiny fists pounding a wall, and as she drew closer, she realized Ruth was in one of the cabins. Pushing the door open, she found her perched atop a bunk bed, a blanket wrapped around her, shivering with fear and from her clothing, which was soaked with the frigid water. "Ruth! Oh, baby, thank God!"

"Aunt Meg! You finded me!"

"I did," Meg assured her as she dropped down into her arms.

"And you found Dolly New Eyes!"

"Come on, baby, let's get you upstairs where it's dry."

※

JONATHAN STOOD near the lifeboats with Kelly, his arm around her in an attempt to keep her and Baby Lizzy as warm as possible. He frequently checked his pocket watch and looked around for any signs of Charlie, Meg, or Daniel. At 12:45, a flare illuminated the sky above them, with the bursting sound of a firecracker, causing many of the children to squeal in delight. It was a sure sign to Jonathan that this was no drill. The ship was going down. "Let's scoot forward a bit, Kelly, shall we?" he asked, guiding her closer to the nearest lifeboat.

Upon reaching a location nearer what happened to be Lifeboat Number 6, Jonathan saw a familiar face. "Molly," he said, getting her attention.

"Well, if it isn't my favorite valet," she smiled. She was dressed in a fur coat and gloves with a hat to match. "Where's Charlie?" she asked, glancing around.

"Looking for Meg."

"And my daughter, Ruth," Kelly added.

"Oh, you must be Kelly," Molly nodded. "It's nice to meet you, though not under these circumstances. I'm Molly Brown. And oh, look at that wee baby. She's precious."

"Thank you," Kelly said, obviously still very distraught.

"Now, don't you worry. If Charlie's lookin' for your girls, I'm sure he'll find 'em. Your husband out, lookin' too?" she asked.

"Yes," Kelly replied, tears in her eyes now.

Molly nodded. "I'm sure they'll all be just fine."

Just then, one of the officers stepped forward and demanded their attention, explaining that they were about to load this lifeboat. Many of the First Class passengers began to groan, but it was quite apparent to others that they needed to get off of *Titanic* in a hurry. The officers worked as quickly as possible to load the boat in an orderly fashion, and when it came her turn to get aboard, Kelly hesitated for a moment. Molly offered to hold Lizzy while she stepped inside, and she handed her over. She turned back for a second, and Jonathan placed his hands around her waist, lifting her over the edge of the boat and into the seat next to Molly who promptly handed her baby back.

Once all of the women and children present were loaded onto the boat, the officer yelled, "Anyone else then!"

Now, it was Jonathan's turn to hesitate. He had gotten Kelly aboard the lifeboat as promised. She was with Molly, which meant that she was safe. He could easily back away now and set off in search of Charlie. Kelly seemed to see the hesitancy in his eyes. "Jonathan!" she yelled. "Get on the boat. You must! If anythin' should happen to you, Ruthy will be beside herself. Please, get on the boat!"

Obviously, Kelly was not able to hold herself together under the circumstances, and when Molly also began to implore him to get on the boat, he took one last look around and climbed in next to another gentleman in the back, praying he didn't regret his decision. If he made it off of *Titanic* alive and Charlie didn't, he would never be able to live with himself.

The officer waited another moment or two, looking around for any other potential lifeboat passengers; since there appeared to be none, he gave the order to lower Lifeboat Number 6 into the Atlantic with only twenty-eight passengers, not even half full.

⚜

MEG WAS SINGING. At this point she wasn't even sure what the song was, but she continued to sing as she searched for a way out because she hoped it would make Ruth feel calmer. However, the muffled sobs coming from beneath the blanket told her it wasn't working. Nevertheless, she continued to sing any tune that came to mind as she made turn after turn, attempting to find any passage at all that might lead to a stairwell or an exit.

She was pretty sure she was on the right track at last, though the water was now up to her waist and she could no longer keep Ruth completely out of it. The blanket was growing heavier and heavier as it retained water, and her arms were burning. But she pressed on. Then, as she turned a corner, she saw it, a stairwell. The water was much deeper here, but the stairwell meant she could return to the more familiar E Deck, and eventually, a way out.

"Come on, baby," she said quietly. "Aunt Meg sees the stairs!" The water at the bottom of the staircase was almost to her chest, and Ruth squealed when the icy water enveloped her. Meg knew the higher she climbed up the stairs, they dryer they would become, so she took off as fast as possible, keeping an eye on the slippery stairs beneath her the best she could in the dim light. That's why she didn't realize there was a gate at the top of the stairs until she had already reached it. With one hand, she gave the gate a shake, clutching Ruth with the other. It didn't budge. "No... no... no... NO! NO! You've got to be kidding me! What else could possibly go wrong?"

As if in answer to her question, there was a sharp banging sound from the floor below them and a flood of water came bursting through the hall they had just exited with a velocity that would have easily knocked her off of her feet had she still been standing there. While she was lucky to have escaped the initial gush, the water in the stairwell was beginning to rise, and now there was no way for her to go back the way she came.

They were trapped against a locked gate.

She knew she couldn't let Ruth see her panic, but she had no idea what to do next. She was determined not to give up, but everything was beginning to look hopeless. "Okay, okay, there's got to be something we can do," she muttered.

"Aunt Meg, why won't you open the gate?" Ruth asked, peering out from around the blanket.

"Because it's locked, darling," she replied as calmly as she could.

"What are we going to do?" Ruth asked innocently.

"Well, first I'm going to put you down, and then I'm going to take this pin out of my hair, and see if I can get it to unlock with this, all right?"

"Okay," Ruth agreed.

Meg hated putting her down in the cold water, which was rising every second and currently reached just above Ruth's knees, but she knew she couldn't do this with one hand, if at all. She pulled a bobby pin from her hair and forced it into the lock, doing her best to try to trip the locking mechanism. She could feel it inside but couldn't quite get it to budge. As the cold water began to hit her calves again, she fought the panic that was rising in the back of her mind and forced herself to stay focused.

"Aunt Meg, can I help?" Ruth asked, clutching her doll.

"Can you think of a way that you can help?" Meg asked, still fighting with the lock and the tears that were threatening to spill over.

"Yes," Ruth replied. "I can yell for Charlie to come and save us."

"All right," Meg agreed, just as the bobby pin snapped in half, both pieces falling to the ground. She banged her head against the gate and gave it a sharp shake in frustration. She had another pin in her hair, and she was willing to try again, but she wondered what was the point? Clearly, this wasn't going to work. Nevertheless, she had to try something, and as she fished another pin out of her hair, she joined in with Ruth's cries, methodically at first, but then she realized, Charlie may have been willing to get on a boat without her, but there was no way he would have climbed aboard a lifeboat without Ruth. And if he wasn't on a lifeboat, he had to be searching for them. With all of her heart, she began to scream, "CHARLIE!" while rattling the gate. Despite the fact that they were on an enormous ship with several decks, and he had no idea where they might be, she began to believe he would find them; he simply had to.

The water continued to rise, and Meg glanced down to see it was almost over Ruth's chest now. Abandoning the blanket, she picked Ruth up and swung her over her shoulder, her cries becoming more frantic now. It had dawned on her that, even if Charlie did find them, the gate would still be locked. She was hoping he would be so desperate to save Ruth he would rip it from the wall. She knew her last hope was beginning to fade now, as the water reached her chest. She glanced back down the stairs, wondering if there was any possibility that she could swim back the other direction, when she heard a sound of motion in the water in the hallway on the other side of the gate.

Though Ruth chanted on, she began to yell, "Hello! Is anyone there? Help us, please! I have a child with me!"

The sound of someone approaching continued to grow closer until she couldn't believe her eyes. "What? Did you give up on me?" he asked, smiling at her.

"Oh, my God! Charlie!" Meg yelled. "I can't believe you found us!"

"Charlie!" Ruth yelled.

"Let's get you out of there," he said.

"It's locked," she reminded him. The water had risen so high, she could no longer even see the keyhole.

"It's a good thing I have this, then," he replied, pulling the gate open and showing her the key he had used to do so.

"A key! Where did you get a key?"

"Come on," he said, taking Ruth out of her arms and pulling her back the way he had come. "We need to get you two to a boat immediately."

The water on E Deck was rising, but they were able to walk out of the deepest part fairly quickly. Charlie seemed to know exactly where he was going, and Meg held onto his hand and let him lead her.

"I need to go back to the stairwell and see if I can find Daniel," she explained.

"No time for that," he said dismissively.

"But I promised him I would."

"I saw him on the Boat Deck. I told him that wouldn't work. Besides, he's probably already searched all of E Deck for you. He can't get to F Deck, so he'll be headed up, which is the way we are going. Hopefully, we'll run into him."

"Is this Scotland Road?" Meg asked, struggling to keep up.

"Yes."

"Should I yell for Daddy now?" Ruth asked innocently.

"I think that would be a great idea," Charlie confirmed for her. "But how about you yell Daniel instead of daddy, all right?"

She nodded and began yelling for her father. They were almost out of the water now, and Charlie led them up another stairwell where they encountered another locked gate, which he was able to get them through.

"Why are the gates locked?" Meg asked.

"I'm not sure," Charlie replied, "but it will make it awfully difficult for the Third Class passengers who stayed below deck to make it to the Boat Deck. Thank God Jonathan gave me this key."

Meg nodded. She had assumed that's where it had come from. "Where is he anyway?" she asked.

"If he did as I told him, he should be out on the Atlantic by now, drifting around with Kelly and Lizzy. Otherwise, I have no idea."

Within a few moments, they reached the First Class Promenade, which was directly below the Boat Deck. As they approached the stairway that led up to where the boats were launching, Ruth changed her screams of "Daniel" to "Daddy" and began to wiggle in Charlie's arms, causing him to pause and he and Meg both to turn around. Sure enough, Daniel was there, off in the distance, peering over the railing at the decks below, his cast the only thing that made them sure of his identity.

Meg took off running after him before he could get away from her, yelling his name as she went. In her soaking wet dress, it was difficult to move as fast as she needed to, and she saw him headed toward the stairs. The last thing she wanted to do was go back downstairs. She knew Charlie was waiting for her at the stairway leading to the Boat Deck, but she had to catch Daniel so that she could get Ruth to safety. Just before he began to descend the stairs, he paused and turned back, as if, perhaps he heard her. She waved her arms in the air and he smiled in recognition. She beckoned for him to come that way, and he began to fight his way through the crowd, moving in her direction.

The first thing he said was, "Where's Ruth?"

"With Charlie. Come on," she replied, panting. She grabbed his hand and began to pull him through the crowd as quickly as she could.

Once they fought their way back to the stairwell, Ruth flung her arms around her father's neck, and he kissed her on the cheek quickly before Charlie yanked her away and began clearing a pathway up the stairs. Oddly enough, there were people trying to come down the stairs as well, and Meg began to realize many of these people were running around with absolutely no direction whatsoever, not even fighting to get aboard the lifeboats. It all appeared to be chaos for chaos' sake.

There was a huge crowd of people all the way forward on the ship, so when they reached the Boat Deck, on the port side, Charlie led them all the way aft where crews were working to launch the last few boats on this side, but the crowds were smaller. "Let's go all the way down, quickly," Charlie directed and the other two followed, Meg clutching his arm as she did so.

Once they reached Lifeboat Number 16, they could see there were about twenty people aboard already with only a few others standing about. "All right, Meg, time to get into the boat," Charlie said, handing Ruth to Daniel.

"Okay," she said, after pausing to catch her breath. "Let's go."

He took her by the arms then so she would turn to face him. "I'm not getting in the boat, Meg," he replied.

Her eyebrows furrowed. "What? Why not? There's plenty of room."

He shook his head. "I'm not going to get on a lifeboat when there are hundreds of women and children still aboard this sinking ship, Meg. What kind of man would I be if I did that?"

Panic began to set in again. "No, Charlie, listen, you have to get on the boat. You saw those people down there. They don't even know which way to go. And they're launching these boats practically empty. There's no way those people are going to make it up here in time. If you don't get on the boat... you'll die."

"Meg, they're going to launch this boat in a minute whether you're on it or not, and there's a little girl right here waiting for you to get on. Stop arguing with me, and get on the boat. I'll find another way."

"Anyone else?" the officer in charge of loading the boat yelled.

"Come on Meg, get on the boat so I can give you Ruth," Daniel said.

"Oh, you're going, too," Charlie said gently pushing Daniel toward the boat.

"But how can I, after what you just said?" Daniel argued.

"You only have one arm, and that little girl needs you. Get on the boat, Daniel," Charlie insisted taking Ruth from him so he could climb in. Though it was getting a bit more crowded than some of the other boats, there was room, and he reluctantly climbed aboard.

Charlie hugged Ruth tightly and kissed her cheek. "You be a good girl, and I'll see you on the big boat in the morning," he said, handing her to her father.

"You're coming, too, right Uncle Charlie?" she asked as she settled against her father's lap, someone else wrapping a dry blanket around her.

"You bet I am. I'll be on the next one, okay, love?"

"Miss?" the officer said, clearly holding the boat just for Meg.

Tears were streaming down her face now. "Charlie, I can't..." she said, shaking her head.

"You can, and you will. I need to focus on taking care of myself now, Meg. If you're here, neither one of us will make it out alive. Get on the boat, and I'll see you in the morning, all right?" He brushed a tear off of her cheek.

Meg glanced at the boat, and then out to sea where she could see several lifeboats already floating. She turned her attention back to Charlie, still shaking her head. "I'm so sorry," she said quietly as she began to sob.

"No, none of that now. You have nothing to be sorry about." He pulled her into his arms one more time, hearing the officer beginning to ready the crew of the boat to launch, and Daniel calling her name. He pushed her back to arm's length, looked her in the eyes, and said, "I love you, Meg. I always will."

Despite the fact that the boat was being lowered, she took his face in her hands and kissed him. He lifted her into the air, his lips still pressed to hers, and dropped her over the railing into the lifeboat where the other passengers helped her down into the seat next to Daniel. "I love you!" she yelled, the tears pouring out now.

He stood at the railing waving, blowing kisses at Ruth who was doing the same, until the boat was in the water and drifting off across the placid surface of the Atlantic.

CHAPTER 17

Several crewmen aboard Lifeboat Number 16 were rowing them away from the *Titanic*, afraid it might suck them down when it went under. The further away they got, the more obvious it became that *Titanic* was floundering quickly now. At this distance, one could easily see just how much of the bow was underwater. Though the water was rising in the stern portion as well, from where Meg sat, it looked as if the frigid Atlantic were about to reach the Boat Deck near the front of the ship.

She had come to the realization pretty quickly after being placed in the lifeboat that there was very little chance that Charlie would survive the sinking, particularly if he refused to get on a lifeboat. She had been counting the launches the best she could from where she sat, and it appeared as if only the collapsibles were left. Though her body had begun to shut down, and therefore her tears had dried up, occasionally, she would shutter violently, and if it weren't for the arm of the strange woman who had moved to sit beside her, bringing a blanket in the process, she was fairly certain she would have completely lost contact with the world around her by now.

Ruth's voice was helpful, as well. The questions may have been disruptive to others around them, but they kept her from sliding away entirely, tempting as it were.

"Daddy, which little boat is Mummy in?

"Well, Mummy was one of the first to go in a little boat, so probably one that is very far away."

"With Baby Lizzy?'

"Yes, love."

"And Mr. Jonaffin?"

"Yes."

She asked question after question, and each one her father fielded handsomely, except for when she'd ask about Charlie.

"Which boat is Uncle Charlie in, Daddy?"

"I'm not sure, darlin'."

"He is in a boat, isn't he, Daddy?"

"Let us pray that he is."

"The water is very cold, isn't' it Daddy?"

"Yes, love."

"I should think it would be hard to swim when one is so cold.

"Yes, darlin'."

"Daddy, do you think, if Uncle Charlie could swim to our boat, we could find a space for him?"

"Perhaps, love. But it would be a very far distance for Uncle Charlie to swim to our boat. I think he shall get in another boat, a closer one."

"Does anyone know the time?" a woman in the back of the boat asked quietly.

"Time to pray," was the answer she received at first.

Then another voice answered, "I have eight past two."

"Why aren't any other ships coming to help?"

"How long shall we drift about out here?"

"I should rather drift about here endlessly than still be on Titanic...."

Meg had begun to chant a prayer over and over in her head, similar to the chant she and Ruth had sent out into the universe not that long —an eternity—ago when they would have died, locked below deck, if Charlie hadn't found them. "Please, God, save Charlie... please, God, save Charlie... please, God, save Charlie...." She repeated it over and over again in her mind, in her heart, begging, pleading, for it to be so. Over the years of abuse, she had attempted to strike a bargain with God so many times. "If you keep him out tonight, I'll contribute to so many charities, help so many in need, say so many prayers..." anything she could think of. Rarely was there any sort of response from the heavens, and over the years she had come to believe God suffered from selective hearing. But the fact that she had found Ruth, and then Charlie had found them, that they were sitting on this lifeboat now, made her think, perhaps, miracles were possible.

And she just needed one more.

Ten minutes after the time had been given, they watched in stunned horror as the water completely covered the Boat Deck from the bow. The lights blinked once, and then went out forever. Even with only the light from the heavens, they could clearly see the stern portion of the ship lifting out of the water. Meg thought she had entirely lost her grip on reality—that what she was seeing could not possibly be real—as the back portion of the boat began to lift into the air. The gasps aboard the lifeboat were hardly audible, but the screams emanating from the ocean liner carried across the expanse now, and many of those around her began to weep in empathy for those who were now surely living the most terrifying experience one could possibly imagine.

Once the tail end of the ship was nearly vertical, there was a gut-wrenching screech as tons of metal and wood began to ratchet apart, the weight of the bow beneath the surface of the water far too great for the aft portion to bear. With a resounding roar, the ship broke into two pieces, and the forward portion of the hull disappeared under the surface of the water.

The tail of the ship came crashing back down then, and even from such a great distance, it was clear to Meg that those tiny specks flying into the ocean were people—men, women, and children who had not been as lucky as she. The screams intensified and then, the tail section floundered as well, tipping up once more before the Atlantic swallowed her whole. There in the distance, in the vast space where the world's greatest ocean liner once stood, was nothing but inky blackness and a few lapping waves.

But then the noises began to intensify, the screams of hundreds, if not thousands, of people in the water. It was hard to distinguish precisely what any of them were saying, but she knew they were begging for help, for the very boats they were sitting in to go back and rescue them, to save the children they so desperately clung to, to assist the injured, to find a way to end the misery of a thousand needles sticking into their bodies as the bone-numbingly frigid water began to chew at their flesh.

"We need to go back," someone behind her was saying.

"There are children out there," said another.

But no one said anything loud enough to make the crewmen act.

And all Meg could say now was the same thing she had been saying for the last fifteen minutes, "Please, God, please save Charlie." Only this time, rather than keeping it as a thought in her head, it became a whisper, and then an almost inaudible gasp while she used up what little voice she had left. Then she realized Ruth was saying it, too, as was Daniel, and she could only hope that somehow, God would heed their cries.

She could see some of the other lifeboats coming together now. Some of the passengers were being moved from one boat to another. And within a few moments, two of the lifeboats began to make their way back toward the wreckage.

"Look, they're going back!"

"They'll help those people in the water."

"They'd better hurry. The cries are dying down. Won't take long to freeze to death in these temperatures."

"Please, God, please save Charlie."

The woman next to her, the one who had her arm around her, she was saying it, too. Meg glanced up at her face for the first time and realized the woman who was doing her best to keep Meg from toppling overboard--both physically and mentally—was none other than Mrs. Appleton.

Meg continued to chant her prayer until her voice ran out completely. Shortly thereafter, the world began to spin, and she leaned her head against Mrs. Appleton's shoulder still pleading for a miracle.

About an hour later, flares from an approaching ship signaled that help was nearby, and sighs of relief from the survivors in the lifeboats resonated around them. It wasn't until approximately 4:10 AM that the *Carpathia* began receiving the occupants of the first of *Titanic*'s twenty lifeboats. The process would take over four hours, and a few of those who had been rescued from the ship, or plucked out of the water, would not make it aboard *Carpathia* alive.

Before the sun came up on April 15, 1912, approximately 1,500 of the 2,250 lives aboard *Titanic* had been lost.

⁂

MEG HAD LOST consciousness somewhere between the dispatch of the two rescue lifeboats and the arrival of the *Carpathia*. It wasn't until Mrs. Appleton shook her softly to let her know it was their turn to mount the ladder to the new ocean liner that she fully came to. Her dress was stiff with ice particles, as was her hair, and as she began to move just to straighten up, every part of her body protested. She glanced over at Ruth, who was sleeping on her father's shoulder, and Daniel managed a small smile. Her initial thought, her continuous thought, was a simple one. I've lost Charlie again. This time, it seemed, it would be for good.

Getting aboard the *Carpathia* required a lot of help, but she managed to do so. Once aboard, the survivors were immediately ushered away from the Boat Deck to the interior of the boat where several public areas had been prepared to receive them. At first, Meg insisted on being allowed to stay on the Boat Deck to watch as the other boats came in, looking for Charlie, of course, but then she realized there had been no rhyme and reason to how the boats were received, and if he had survived, he could well be aboard the *Carpathia* already. The crew of the *Carpathia* was doing their best to calm the distraught passengers, and as such they had some rules and guidelines they were trying to keep in place to prevent a mass of hysterical women from clogging up the Boat Deck. Therefore, Meg, Daniel, and Ruth were ushered away with Mrs. Appleton and the rest of the survivors from Lifeboat Number 16.

Meg's head seemed quite foggy as she entered the dining lounge where the majority of the *Titanic* survivors were being attended to. She glanced around, but her vision was blurry. Despite being inside at last, she still felt quite cold.

"Here, love, take this hot tea," a kind woman said, approaching her from behind and wrapping a fresh blanket around her as she handed her the mug. "Oh dear, you're frozen solid!" she declared upon seeing the ice crystals on the bottom of Meg's dress. "Come with me," she insisted.

Meg glanced around and saw that another woman was carrying Ruth off, presumably for the same reason, Daniel behind her, and though Meg didn't particularly want to be separated from her family, she had no voice to argue, so she plodded along behind on rubbery legs.

A few moments later, the woman had assisted her in changing to dry, warm clothing, forced a second beverage upon her, wrapped her up in that fresh blanket, and escorted her back out to the holding area. "Have a seat, love, and I'll see if I can't track down your family."

As she turned to walk away, Meg's hand shot out, and she grabbed her arm. "Charles Ashton."

"What's that, love?" the woman said bending closer. "Your voice is so hoarse, I can hardly understand you."

"Charles Ashton," she repeated.

The woman straightened a bit. "The millionaire?" she asked. Meg nodded. The woman's forehead creased a bit. "Not rightly sure, love, but I'll find out." Meg forced a small smile and drew her hand back under the blanket. "Sit tight, sweetheart. I think I see my friend who had your husband and little girl right over there."

That would explain the odd look, Meg thought, but with no words to correct the misunderstanding, she did as she was told, pouring all of her concentration into thawing her body so that she could begin her search for Charlie.

"Meg!" she must have dozed off again. When she opened her eyes, she was looking into a familiar pair, and though they were not quite the ones she had longed to see, she was still happy to see them.

"Jonathan!" She jumped out of the chair and threw her arms around his neck, only realizing too late how painful such quick, random movements could be. "You're safe, then?" she said, ignoring the shooting pain in her arms and shoulders.

"Yes, Kelly, Lizzy and I made it aboard *Carpathia* several hours ago. I've been looking for you. How are you?" he asked, an expression of concern on his face.

"I think I'm all right," she assured him. "Have you..."

"No," he shook his head sharply. "I was hoping, perhaps, you could indicate where he might be. I attempted to speak with Daniel, but he was in so much pain from his arm, and Kelly was doting over him and Ruth so much, I began to search for you instead. No one aboard *Carpathia* has been able to tell me anything."

Meg was happy to hear that the O'Connell family had been reunited. "I'm afraid I know as little as you do," she explained.

"You didn't see which way he went after he got off of the lifeboat?" Jonathan clarified.

Meg stared at him for a moment. He had no idea. "Daniel didn't tell you? Jonathan, Charlie didn't get on the lifeboat with us."

"What?" he asked his eyes doubling in size. "What do you mean?"

"He refused. He said he couldn't get on a lifeboat when there were women and children going down with the ship." Repeating his words from those final moments together was extremely painful, and she found herself sinking back into the deck chair she had been occupying previously.

Jonathan collapsed to his knees beside her. "But—if he didn't get aboard a lifeboat...."

Tears began to overflow from her eyes again, and she squeezed them tight against the reality of his words.

He was quiet for a moment, only shaking his head slowly from time to time. Eventually, he said, "I thought for sure when I saw Daniel and Ruth that you'd all made it aboard safe...."

"I tried..." she began.

"Oh, no, Meg," Jonathan stopped her, placing his hand on top of hers. "You mustn't blame yourself. If Charlie had his mind set on some-thing, trust me, there was no changing it."

She hated that he was using past tense already. "Was there anyone... anyone at all... from the water?"

Jonathan's disposition changed and a miniscule glimmer of hope appeared for just a second before being snuffed away. "I'm honestly not quite sure. I had been paying attention to what they were saying about the lifeboats. I know there were a few people taken directly to the medical station, those that were pulled from the collapsibles, I believe. Let me go do some checking, and I will come back and tell you what I discover."

"No."

"Pardon?"

"I'll come with you," she said, pulling herself to her unsteady feet.

"Meg, you're pale as death. You need to rest."

"What I need... is Charlie."

"Very well then."

As she took her first few steps, overwhelming pain shot through her feet and up through her legs. She wondered if, perhaps, she didn't have some frostbite. But with each step, the pain dulled, and soon she was able to make some semblance of a normal gait. Jonathan had offered his arm, and she could tell he was growing a bit impatient with her as she struggled to keep up, but as she grew stronger, her speed increased, and soon he began to tug on her less as they made their way through the throng of people.

"Do you want to speak to Kelly first? She's just over there?" he asked gesturing across the crowd.

Meg could see her friend and her family off in the distance. Though Daniel was very pale, Ruth was dancing around her mother's feet, and Baby Lizzy was cooing at her. She caught Kelly's eyes and held them for a second, a small smile flashing between them. "No," she replied. "Later."

Jonathan seemed relieved and pressed on. "I'm not quite sure who to ask that might know something—anything—new. I've asked all those taking names, the people with the clipboards."

"But no one ever asked my name," she assured him. It was still possible to have boarded the *Carpathia* without being on the list.

"True, I couldn't find you either. But there was a Meg West listed right after Daniel O'Connell, and I thought perhaps that was you."

She smiled, realizing Daniel must have made up an alias for her.

"Perhaps it is," she replied. "If you've checked with all of these folks, then let's try the hospital you spoke of."

"Very well," he consented. "I do believe they are being very careful not to disturb the patients, however. Rumor has it that a few of those in the worst shape have already expired since they were brought aboard."

Jonathan asked a member of the *Carpathia* crew which way to the hospital, and while he was willing to give them directions, he said, "There are only a few male patients there and one female. Crowds of people looking for their lost loved ones are trying to get a glimpse of who might be inside, but the medical crew is being very protective of the patients."

"We're looking for Charles Ashton," Meg explained. "Do you know him?"

"Know him? Of course, I know him. But, no, I haven't seen him. Guggenheim. Astor. Straus. Hell, I've even been asked about Morgan. But I haven't seen any of them," the young man replied. "If you're just looking for an autograph or a hand out..."

"I'm his fiancée."

The boy bit his tongue. "Pardon, Miss Westmoreland. I didn't recognize you."

"It's quite all right," she assured him. "And whatever you do, don't add my name to that list."

"Yes, miss. I hope you find him."

"Come along, Meg," Jonathan said, pulling her in the direction he had indicated.

When they reached the hospital, they were able to confirm the boy's description of pandemonium. The *Carpathia* crew was doing their best to calm the seas of people who were stopping by to see if missing loved ones had been taken to the hospital, but most of them were being turned away in tears. As they approached, Meg overheard a woman wearing a nurse's hat saying, "I'm sorry, madam, but the only men inside the hospital are First and Second Class passengers or *Titanic* crew member. There are no members of Steerage in the hospital."

The woman, who appeared to be Slovakian and possibly spoke little English was repeating herself, "My husband. Please."

Meg's heart was breaking for this woman and so many others who were desperately searching for their lost spouses and loved ones. She knew the hospital was the last hope for them—as it was for her—and the fear that she might soon be joining them in their misery was an ever-growing concern.

"Pardon me," Jonathan was saying to a crew member who was still occupied with a woman begging him to "check one more time." The older man looked relieved to at least have someone else to interact with. "We're looking for Charles Ashton. I'm his valet. Do you happen to know if he's in the hospital?"

"No," the gentleman said curtly.

"No, he's not, or no you don't know?" Jonathan asked for clarification.

"No, I don't know," the man said a bit kindlier. "I know there are a few First Class passengers inside, but most of them are unconscious, or barely conscious, and we haven't identified all of them."

"Surely you must know what he looks like," Jonathan pressed.

The man scoffed. "Well, if he's in that room, he looks pale and blue."

"That's not funny," Meg hissed. "Whoever those men are, their families are out here looking for them."

The crewmen seemed to realize his folly. "I'm sorry," he said solemnly. "That was uncalled for. I honestly don't know what Mr. Ashton looks like, but I will go inside and see if anyone can identify him now that we know there's a possibility he might be among the patients."

"Thank you," Meg said quietly.

The crewmen disappeared into the crowd. When he opened the door to the hospital to squeeze through, the throngs of people pressed forward, several of the women outside attempting to gain a peek. It seemed like ages before the door opened again. Meg was beginning to grow dizzy, and she was thankful for Jonathan's arm around her. The wails of the women and children nearby were growing unbearable.

Even before the man reached them, he was shaking his head, an indicator that Charlie was not inside the hospital. "Sorry, sir, miss. He's not in there."

"Are you sure?" Meg asked, tears stinging her eyes.

"I'm sure. One of the nurses says she knows precisely what Mr. Ashton looks like. She even peeled open the sleeping patients' eyes to check their color, just to double-check. That's what took so long. He ain't here. I apologize."

"Is there anywhere else..." Meg began, not quite ready to give up hope yet.

"Miss..."

"I don't think so," the man replied. "As far as I know, the only intensive care patients are in the hospital. If he's not in the lounge..."

"Miss..."

"...and he's not in here, it's likely..."

"MISS!"

"...he didn't make it...."

As he was completing his sentence, Meg felt a sharp tug on her shoulder, and she turned to see the woman who had helped her change her dress earlier in the day. The look on her face made Meg catch her breath.

"I found 'im."

CHAPTER 18

"You what?" Meg asked, not sure she'd heard correctly.

"I found 'im. I found Mr. Ashton, like you asked. I've been lookin' everywhere for you," she continued.

Meg looked from the woman to Jonathan and back again. "What? Where? Are you sure? Is he...."

"Come along, then," she said leading the way out of the crowd and back the other direction toward the First Class passengers' cabins.

"Most of the crew don't know the doctor arranged for a few of the more critical, higher priority patients, if you will, to have their own cabins. The doctor's been so busy, as you can imagine. The whole medical crew has been...."

Meg was hurrying to keep up with her. "Are you saying he's alive then?" she asked once again.

"To the best of my knowledge," she replied, "though the gal I talked to said he wasn't doing so well, and that was an hour ago. If we hurry, you might make it in time."

"In time?"

"To say goodbye."

☙❧

THERE WERE VOICES AGAIN, soft ones, distant ones. He couldn't understand them. It was if they were speaking into glass jars, or wads of cotton. Once in a while, he would catch a word or two. "Hot water bottle," "warm wrap," "amputation," "expiration." He had no idea who or what they were talking about. He didn't know where he was or what he was doing. All he knew was that he needed to find a way to open his eyes, to look for... someone..., but each eyelid seemed to weigh a cubic ton, and even when he did manage to force them open, he could only keep them slitted for a moment, and he could only make out shapes and forms.

And then everything would go black again, and the welcome warmth of oblivion would overtake him. Existing was becoming more painful than he could bear. It would be so much easier just to stop.

He was contemplating that idea again when a new voice caught his attention, and then another. They both seemed familiar somehow, though he couldn't be sure, what with the speakers insisting on muffling every word. For the first time, he was fairly certain he heard his own name, followed by a mumbled response, the only words of which he caught were, "not long now."

What would not be long now? Would the boats be back soon? Then, he remembered; the boats were there. He wasn't floating on the collapsible anymore. Perhaps the man meant they would be arriving in New York soon. Or maybe Meg would be there soon. There it was—that's what he was trying to remember. Meg. How could he forget? He needed to find Meg.

As if summoned by angels, he heard her voice again then. It had been that sweet sound which had caught his attention only a moment ago. But it was closer now, hovering above him. She sounded upset. He was hopeful she had not been injured aboard the lifeboat. The lifeboat. Meg had been on a different lifeboat. He had been holding on for dear life, for hours, trying to get back to her. Now, here she was. But something was wrong.

He focused on her words with all of his might. "Get better," she was saying. "Soon." Perhaps she was saying he would be all better soon. That would be welcome. He should very much like to get better soon.

The pain in his hands had subsided the longer he had been laying here, and he began to wonder if they hadn't given him some medicine. He felt Meg's small, smooth hand on his, and even though it stung when she squeezed his fingers, it was nice. He just wished he could open his eyes so he could look at her, but try as he might, his eyes refused to open.

She was saying his name again, and it was melodic. There were other people talking, too, but he focused only on Meg. Beautiful Meg. To think, he'd almost walked away from her forever over a silly misunderstanding. None of that mattered now. She was here. And he would be better soon. She had said so.

He felt a burning sensation in his lungs. This was a new development, and he began to wonder if perhaps she had placed something heavy on his chest. He had no idea why she might do such a thing, but then, not a lot was making sense just now. He attempted to ignore the unpleasantness and returned his focus to her angelic voice. What was she saying? Oh, yes, Ruth. That little spitfire. He couldn't wait to see her again. She sure had caused some trouble getting off of that boat. He should like to take her to see the dawfins off Coney Island someday soon. She would like that. Perhaps she would even want to ride the roller coaster.

There was that burning again. The worst part was, it was making it nearly intolerable to breathe. He could still feel Meg's hand on his, but for some reason, it seemed as if she were backing away, her voice growing fainter and fainter. Why would she leave? Surely, she'd stay with him until he was able to open his eyes and look at her.

The feeling of floating was back now. But the water must have been warmer this time because the stabbing sensation from before, when he was holding tight to the collapsible, was gone. In fact, all of the pain in his body was beginning to fade, all of it except for the burning in his lungs. That seemed to be morphing a bit, as if his lungs were turning into something else. Maybe he was developing gills.... No, that wasn't it. Where was Meg going? Why wouldn't she stay with him? He could barely understand her now.

She was saying his name. Of that, he was certain. And she was saying it louder, almost the way she had been saying it when she was calling him to help her get through the gate. She sounded almost as frantic. But there was something else. What was it? "Stay." "No." Was she saying she couldn't stay? "Love you." Now that he heard. Perhaps she would just be gone a little while, and then she would come back. All was well. He just needed to rest a bit longer, to find a way to open his eyes, stop the burning, and the floating....

"Charlie! Charlie! No, please, stay with me! I love you so much. Please!" Meg was begging now, her head on his chest, sobbing uncontrollably.

The doctor was there again now, checking for a pulse. "Miss Westmoreland," he said quietly, "I'm sorry. I'm afraid he's gone."

Meg sat up sharply. "No," she pleaded. "You don't understand. I just found him."

"I assure you, we've done everything we can, even before you arrived...."

He didn't understand. She didn't mean literally. Now, after all of these years of suppositions and misguided loathing, she had finally substantiated the gift her father had granted her even before his death in prearranging not just a marriage, but an unparalleled, life-long gift of undying love and devotion. What's more, despite the fact that she could not bear to think of her own life without him, Charlie deserved to live. He had risked his own life in order that so many others would have a chance to survive. He was kind, and good, and loving, and perfect in so many, many ways. And she refused to believe he could slip away from her—from them—so easily.

"Do something, please," she pleaded.

The doctor looked at her sympathetically. "If there was anything I could do, Miss Westmoreland, I assure you, I would do it. But I'm not a miracle worker. Take a moment and say your goodbyes," he added, looking from her to Jonathan who was standing at the foot of the bed.

Meg stared down at him through tear-blurred eyes, her body heaving, each breath a struggle. "I'm so sorry, Charlie," she whispered. "I should have made you get on the boat. I should have prayed harder." She began to realize there was nothing more that she could say, nothing she could do, and the feel of Jonathan's hand on her back indicated he thought she needed to go. She couldn't imagine walking away from Charlie again. She didn't think she could do it. She began to wish she'd stayed aboard the *Titanic* as well.

"Come along, Meg," Jonathan said quietly. "Ruth will be missing you."

Of course, there was Ruth. She needed to be strong for Ruth. She nodded, though she still could not tear her gaze from his handsome face. Even in death, his skin pale, his lips blue, he was still so very handsome. "I can't let go yet, Jonathan," she said quietly.

"All right then," he said quietly. "I'll... go talk to Daniel and Kelly."

Meg realized this had to be incredibly difficult for Jonathan as well. Perhaps he needed to be alone, to mourn in his own way. And that was fine. He could go off to mourn if that's what he needed. But she wasn't ready to give up. Not yet.

She leaned in next to Charlie's ear and whispered, "I love you, Charlie," and pressed her lips against his, lingering long enough so that she would never forget the feel of him.

She was just about to tear herself away when she realized not only were his lips warm, they seemed to be growing warmer. At first, she thought it must be her imagination, but then she realized it wasn't—and he was trying to kiss her back. She pulled away just a bit to look at him and saw his eyelid twitch. "Charlie?" she asked, cautiously. His reply was another eyelid twitch. "Charlie!" she said again.

One of the nurses was pulling on her arm now. "Miss Westmoreland, he's gone. You need to accept that."

"No, he just moved his eyelid," she insisted.

"I'm sure it's just a muscle spasm," she said quietly.

As she watched, his eyelids began to flutter. "Get the doctor," she ordered.

"Miss..."

"Get the doctor!"

She did as she was told, and Meg watched as Charlie attempted to open his eyes. Instinctively, she tried the one thing that had worked so well last time and pressed her lips against his again. She was certain he was trying to kiss her back this time for sure. She heard the door open behind her and momentarily pulled away to say to the doctor, "Check his pulse again."

There was a deep sigh as he crossed over to the bed. "Miss West-moreland, the body twitches and spasms as the tissues begin to expire," he explained.

"Please, just check."

The doctor took Charlie's wrist in his hand, and immediately his countenance changed. "I'll be damned," he muttered.

"He's alive, isn't he?" Meg asked, the faintest flicker of hope still before her.

"Yes, he is," the doctor assured her. "In fact, I think this is the strongest his pulse has been since they brought him in. Nurse, let's change these warmers," he said, gently laying Charlie's arm back on the bed.

Meg leaned back in next to his ear. She could distinctly hear him breathing now. "Charlie," she said quietly. "Thank you. Thank you for coming back to me. Please, don't ever leave me again. I couldn't bear it. Now, please focus on getting better. You must find a way to stay with me."

The nurses were bustling about, following the doctor's instructions. Meg moved slightly out of the way when she needed to, but she never let go of his hand, and by the time they were done, he had quite a bit of color back in his face. His lips were no longer blue, and the flut-tering in his eyelids was substantial.

Meg sat on the edge of his bed, praying softly, holding his hand, waiting for what seemed like an eternity. She truly felt like this was worse than the hours she spent in the lifeboat. The miracle was finally brought to complete fruition when Charlie whispered her name. Eyes widened, she leaned in next to his ear. "Charlie, I'm right here. Can you open your eyes?" she asked.

His eyelids fluttered and then there they were, those gorgeous green eyes. He looked a bit confused at first, but she didn't give him an opportunity to say anything before she kissed him, and despite his potential delirium, he returned the kiss, squeezing her hand as he did so.

"Oh, my God, Charlie," she said as she finally pulled away. "We lost you. You were gone."

He gazed up at her, a small smile playing at the corner of his lips. "Well, I'm here now," he assured her.

Once again she was fighting back tears, but this time they were tears of joy. "Promise me you'll never leave me again."

"I promise," he said quietly. "Will you do the same?"

"Yes, of course," she said as he slowly reached up to brush a wayward tear from her cheek.

"And when we reach America, will you be my wife at last?"

"Nothing in the world could stop me."

She leaned in and kissed him again and the feel of his arms around her assured her that they were finally safe. "I love you, Charlie," she said, smiling down at him.

"I love you, too, Meg. More than anything. Thank you for saving my life."

"Thank you for saving mine," she replied. She rested her head gently on his shoulder, so grateful to have him back. She whispered, "Thank you for saving Charlie."

"What was that?" he asked.

"Nothing," she replied, "just showing some gratitude."

He seemed to understand. After a moment, he said, "Meg?"

"Yes, love?"

"When we go on our honeymoon, can we take a train?"

She began to laugh in spite of everything. "Yes," she assured him. "An old, small, slow train."

"What could possibly go wrong?" he muttered before leaning down and kissing her gently on the forehead.

Laying in his arms, Meg was hopeful that all of her years of hardship were over at last and that she could begin her new life with Charlie in New York, leaving the ghosts of Southampton far behind.

The End

If you'd like to keep reading, you can find Book 2, *Residuum* on Amazon by clicking on the title.
Prelude, the prequel is also available on Amazon.

A NOTE FROM THE AUTHOR....

Dear Reader,

Typing the words "the end" at the conclusion of *Ghosts of Southampton: Titanic* was both triumphant and disheartening. Like all of the characters I have created, Meg and Charlie have truly claimed a place in my heart, and I hope you enjoyed reading their story as much as I enjoyed telling it. I am happy to say this is not the ultimate end for this pair. You can read about what happens once the ship docks in New York City in *Residuum*. I have also written prequel, *Prelude*, so that readers can gain a little more insight into exactly what transpired before Meg and Charlie boarded *Titanic* that fateful morning in April.

If you would, please leave an honest review of *Ghosts of Southampton: Titanic* on your retailer's product page.

Additionally, you may enjoy some of my other titles listed in the "Also by ID Johnson" section.

I'd love to stay in touch! You can download *Leaving Ginny*, an historical romance novelette based on *Beneath the Inconstant Moon* on Instafreebie when you sign up for my newsletter. Here is the link: https://claims.instafreebie.com/free/Eypqj

Once again, thank you so much for taking the time to read my book!

Best regards,
ID Johnson

ALSO BY ID JOHNSON:

Stand Alone Titles

Deck of Cards

(steamy romance)

Cordia's Will: A Civil War Story of Love and Loss

(clean romance/historical)

The Doll Maker's Daughter at Christmas

(clean romance/historical)

Beneath the Inconstant Moon

(literary fiction/historical psychological thriller)

Pretty Little Monster

(young adult/suspense)

The Journey to Normal: Our Family's Life with Autism *(nonfiction)*

The Clandestine Saga series

(paranormal romance)

Transformation

Resurrection

Repercussion

Absolution

Illumination

Destruction

Annihilation

A Vampire Hunter's Tale (based on The Clandestine Saga)

(paranormal/alternate history)

Aaron

Jamie

Elliott

The Chronicles of Cassidy (based on The Clandestine Saga)

(young adult paranormal)

So You Think Your Sister's a Vampire Hunter?

Who Wants to Be a Vampire Hunter?

How Not to Be a Vampire Hunter

My Life As a Teenage Vampire Hunter

Vampire Hunting Isn't for Morons

Ghosts of Southampton series

(historical romance)

Prelude

Titanic

Residuum

Heartwarming Holidays Sweet Romance series

(Christian/clean romance)

Melody's Christmas

Christmas Cocoa

Winter Woods

Waiting On Love

Shamrock Hearts

A Blossoming Spring Romance

Firecracker!

Falling in Love

Thankful for You

Melody's Christmas Wedding

The New Year's Date

Reaper's Hollow

(paranormal/urban fantasy)

Ruin's Lot

Ruin's Promise

Ruin's Legacy

Collections

Ghosts of Southampton Books 0-2

Reaper's Hollow Books 1-3

The Clandestine Saga Books 1-3

For updates, visit www.authoridjohnson.blogspot.com

Follow on Twitter @authoridjohnson

Find me on Facebook at www.facebook.com/IDJohnsonAuthor

Instagram: @authoridjohnson

Amazon: ID Johnson

Made in the USA
San Bernardino, CA
30 August 2019